THE HOUSE
OF ORDER

JOHN PAUL JARAMILLO

ANAPHORA LITERARY PRESS

COCHRAN, GEORGIA

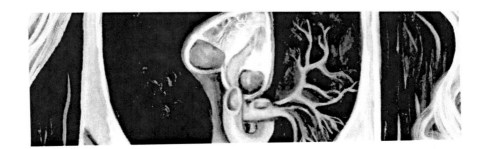

ANAPHORA LITERARY PRESS
163 Lucas Rd., Apt. I-2
Cochran, GA 31014
www.anaphoraliterary.wordpress.com

Book design by Anna Faktorovich, Ph.D.

Cover Illustration: "Breathe Out" by Felicia Olin
Cover Design: Thom Whalen

Published in 2011 by Anaphora Literary Press

The House of Order
John Paul Jaramillo—1st edition.

ISBN-13: 978-1-937536-16-9
ISBN-10: 1937536165

Library of Congress Control Number: 2011945742

THE HOUSE OF ORDER

JOHN PAUL JARAMILLO

ACKNOWLEDGMENTS

For my D. For my family.

"Farmhouse in the Lanes" has appeared online at the *Acentos Review*; "Little Blue Box" online at *Antique Children Arts Journal*; "Driven to the Fields" has appeared in the *Antique Children Arts Quarterly*; "Rabbit Story" in the *Copper Nickel Review*; "Laundromat Story" online at *Crash Literary Journal*; "Penance" online at *Verdad Magazine*; "Descansos" has appeared in *Paraphilia Magazine* and "Grown-Ass Men" in *Sleet Magazine*.

Cover Artwork: "Breathe Out" by Felicia Olin.

CONTENTS

1. RABBIT STORY

"**Y**ou can't tell a man's story unless you are for sure about the facts, Manito." In the narrow length of the backyard my *Tio* Neto puts out his cigarette with the tips of his fingers and throws the *vacha*. Since the *Abuelito* topped the tree there is not much shade so Neto slaps at the pocket on his chest for sunglasses. "I was eight," he tells me. "No, nine. Hell if I know." He licks at the burns to his fingers.

Neto has just come to the *Abuelita's* from his work laying tar on the old highway, the first job he's held in months. His work shirt hangs open out over his jeans, bare chest exposed.

"I'm tired of telling you these stories," he says.

He goes over to the *truckito* and pulls a lawn chair from the bed. Neto's thick, middle-aged body slams down and he scrapes his cap from a sweaty head and brow. I imagine Neto sits and talks the way his *Jefe* sat and sold similar stories.

"I don't have time to tell such things," he says. He reminds me he is not my father; he reminds me my father is dead. "I was just a little *moco*. The story goes I was out here at two a.m. sleepwalking."

Or maybe pretending and then his father caught him. Maybe Neto happened on the old man sobbing. Even now, decades later, this part I'm not too sure about. What is clear is that he expected to find one of his *Jefe's* girlfriends.

There was the young Martinez girl with the lisp and the flat ass. Or the older lady married to *Tio* Freddie who lived on the east side and carried a clip loaded .45 pistol in her Buick. Maybe the teacher from Goat Hill who lived with her parents. Neto knew of them all.

"I busted him with a girl all kinds of times. He was always with some fine young thing from the neighborhood," Neto says. "You can't blame him too much, you know."

The old man hustled his girlfriends where he kept his tools and where he kept his *truckito*, out near the alley. I know this because Neto knows this.

"I saw everything. The old man right there in the garage throwing *palo*. It was something for a boy."

I ask, "And he never saw you before that night, Neto?"

"No, Manito. Never once caught on."

At one time it was all Neto thought of. Probably became the reason to walk and listen.

"The old man needed his sex. I ain't no pervert but I needed to see, you know," Neto says. "For myself."

That particular night, the night Neto was caught, the "fine young thing" ended up dead-meat and gone and so the man was deserted.

"He always drank when he was deserted," Neto explains.

He gets away from the story to remind me how around Huérfano County "deserted" means losing a ride out to the lanes for work in the onion fields. Quitting school to work and contribute to the mortgage. Ignitions that won't fire and friends who won't come around. Cousins dropped off from New Mexico to share beds and food. Half fixed televisions for Saturday morning cartoons and radios smashed before the World Series. Couches and chairs dropped onto back porches gone un-mended and machine parts and tools sacrificed to the rust of early winters. Here it means CF&I Steel picking up and closing offices, union negotiation talks breaking down. Husbands who aren't faithful. Fathers dying. Lies and stories half-told and then forgotten unless pressed and pushed.

"'Complications of childbirth' is exactly what I read, Manito," Neto continues. "That part is God's truth and factual. You can show the people if you want."

Years later, sitting in the public library, I read it too on page one of the Pueblo Chieftain from July 18th 1963:

"Woman Dies During Childbirth, Family Alleges Negligence by Doc"

That night the old man was crying and "disoriented." Made Neto beg and promise, squeal with pain.

"I mean my *Jefe* was a *cabrón* when he drank," Neto explains. "We all are. You know."

After he caught the boy, my *Abuelito* made the young Neto work picking up leaves. It was late but the *Abuelito* made Neto "police call" the area. That's what the old man named it. From sad Army days, I imagine.

He made him clean up the chicken and rabbit cages the family kept. The whole neighborhood raised them. It was all about him being real *flojo* and saving dollar bills.

"It was all different back then. Not like today with kids all spoiled and shit. You wouldn't survive a day back in the old neighborhood," Neto says.

So there was little Neto, police calling. The *Abuelito* watching him and becoming more and more drunk on his beer or his rum and RC Cola. Or maybe he was drinking his wine. *Abuelita* called him a wino later and so I imagine the *Viejo* from those old photos standing in his bare feet and drinking from a bottle.

"Don't be so stupid, Manito, and listen to the story," Neto says. "You always getting in the way of the story with those little things."

I ask, "Is the story the girl?"

"No, Manito. The story is me and them rabbits."

Abuelito found his rabbits missing and became enraged. Any other night the old man wouldn't have even noticed. He would have walked right past those cages and fucked his little *chingita* in the garage and afterwards pissed on the side of the house.

But his woman had died in a bed at St Mary Corwin giving birth to a daughter, to Neto's sister. To be precise, another young Martinez girl, but he keeps that from the family.

"That's the way it works, Manito. That's what it is to be a man. You'll find out," Neto says. "Some things you got to keep inside. But like I say the story isn't about the girl."

I imagine the *Abuelito* was repeating over and over, "*You want to go under the house, Neto?*" In his white t-shirt and this little cap that made him look like Marlon Brando's character in *The Wild One*, he asked the boy again and again to get under the house.

"*No, Jefe,*" little Neto said. "*I'm sleeping.*"

"*What the hell do you mean you're sleeping, Neto?*" he said. "*Wake your ass up. Get in the Goddamn crawl space and get those Goddamn rabbits.*" *Abuelito* had little Neto's neck in one hand and his bottle in the other. "*I'm not asking you, Neto,*" he said. "*I'm fucking telling you.*"

"*I don't want to, Jefe.*"

"*Goddamn it, boy. I'm telling you to do it. Do you want to be a man, Neto? Do you?*"

Neto didn't want to be a man but he didn't want to wake the *Jefita*, either, and so little Neto fell to his knees and entered the crawl space. The entrance was only a 16" wide black hole. And somehow he found strength and fire from deep inside.

"*Hurry you ass up, Neto,*" the old man said through stained teeth and dirty moustache. "*I ain't got all night.*"

Neto had never seen such darkness, a thousand years of ghosts for a boy. And in that moment Neto became a horrible thought. He never wanted to scream so loudly. His legs trembled and his pajama top was soaked through and dripping.

I ask, "Were you scared, Neto?"

"The *Jefita*, Manito. Think of your Grandmother. She was sleeping. My poor, poor mother."

So Neto crawled and struggled to the darkest corner of his mind past black widows and *ratones*. The fear and yellow bile built in his mouth and in the corners of his lips.

"Big *ratones*, Manito," Neto says. "You've never seen such in your life."

"Goddamn it, Neto," the *Abuelito* said. *"Don't let those ratones get to them rabbits. Them rabbits are sold."*

I ask, "So what did you do, Neto?"

"I grabbed and held them in my hands, Manito," Neto says. "I was bit and everything."

"Then what?"

"And then there was nothing. What do you want to hear, Manito?"

"How could a boy do that?"

"I did it for the *Jefita*. My poor mother. I had to protect her. So don't ask me no more, Manito. Let me sit in peace."

I ask, "What did my father think of all this?"

"Well, I say Goddamn. Now I know you're growing, Manito. Now I know you're nearly what a man should be. A man has got to know about his family."

Then he ignores me. Escapes my questions for cartons of cigarettes stored in the *Abuelita's* Frigidaire and endless cans of RC Cola mixed with rum. Neto's father dead for years now and the family story going the boy killed rats with bare hands, how he mangled and smashed at whatever he could touch.

And later I'll go to sleep with it all deep inside of me. Down in the basement the old man dug out. The same one that took three loads of earth moved to create. That took *Tio* Freddie's *truckito* and cases and cases of beer.

"That part," Neto swears, "is God's truth and factual. So you better get that down in the story." And I promise him I will.

2. FAMILY ALBUM

My Uncle Neto is so far from himself in those photos. The old folks say the same, "Your *Tio* was something in them days, Manito."

His wide, round face so much fresher in those pictures, dark hair close cropped.

"We all look good when we are young," the folks say as they drink and play their Sunday cards. "Don't know what happens."

"No," my *Abuelita* says, "Not just that. My little man was a looker."

In one picture he's leaning up against a bicycle and grabbing onto a bag of marbles. In another he has his *Tio* Mitedio's cowboy hat and he's been out playing with the foster kids and his brother Relles, leading them around the neighborhood from the construction site to the elementary school's gravel basketball court. Down to the jungle gym and trash piles.

In another I study Neto's boyhood home. The mortgaged house with windows on the west side painted shut and blacked over, the windows on the east without screens. Just barely enough grass and vegetation in the back to be called a yard, mostly old machine and rusted engine parts litter the walk out to the garage and *Jefe*'s tools. The breeze sweeps the laundry hanging out on the lines and reveals the small statue of *La Virgen de Guadalupe* and the ancient wagon wheels my *Abuelita* saved from San Luis, Colorado. I imagine the smell of *calabacitas* with fresh corn frying and green *chiles* roasting on the air. In the late afternoons it looks just light enough to make out the cracking, water damaged shingles on the garage and house.

They go on to tell me 1815 Spruce Street never exists in those old photos. As if the collective memory of the family and of little Neto broke down and the only thing left is to recreate in their stories.

Even the *Abuelita* needs the smell of warm pots of *bolita* beans and burning tobacco to remember those years. Whenever a thought comes up the *Compadres* tell her, "No, *Jefita*. It never happened that way. You made that up from your head."

The old folks don't remember. They deny and laugh. "The boys never had it that hard," they say. "You should've seen us back in the day in New Mexico. You wanna see poor? These boys had a roof and yard, food in their bellies. So what the hell did they have to complain about?"

In the only Polaroid in the stack, Neto and his crew sat in the living room, the television drowning out their *Jefita* and the *Jefe*. White crackling static and music of local advertisements filled the air. The boys kept the time of day by cartoons and the Lone Ranger. Neto's *Jefita* kept dinner until after the local newscast and his *Jefe* marked the start of his shift by national news. The boys watched the TV faces and listened closely as they shoveled beans and fried potatoes to their mouths.

I imagine the *Jefita* remembers only the living room in detail and the sounds of the television bouncing off the walls to her inner ears. All the family moments worth talking about are from the living room and the television with her boys lying in socked feet and dirtied undershirts.

The *Jefita* remembers in the summer of 1963 or perhaps, only in her mind, the house and the crew of boys were buried under the neighborhood and nearly disappeared. Lost behind a steel mill, just blocks away.

The family says, "Those boys were some kind of a crew for the *Jefita* to have to deal with, Manito. I don't know how she did it."

She remembers standing in the kitchen and hearing all the noises of the house drowned out by the pressure cooker. The crackling of lard and corn tortillas, and the screaming of boys and fosters drowning out her thoughts.

Neto remembers thinking how he was a small part of a larger hurt around him. He doesn't know for sure how old he was when his eyes were opened.

Maybe when the *Jefe* stepped on his spread of comic books with his steel toes or maybe when the *Jefe* with leathery hands picked up his boy and held him too tightly, the smell of alcohol on his breath. "Get those toys out of the road," the *Jefe* said. "Don't you have any work?"

The crew of fosters crying and laughing as they wrestled and fought for left-over tortillas to the point of bashed foreheads and scratched faces.

On those occasions the *Jefita* walked in and switched off the television. She stared out past the living room filled with pillows, blankets and the *Jefe's* sleeping bag zipped wide open. No expression on her face upon finding crashed glass and spilled blood.

The *Compadres* say to me, "She put them all in their place with a look, Manito." Then she went back to her magazines and her mirror.

Back to her letter writing or long-distance phone calls to the sister in Denver. She escaped any time she could.

On those nights when the *Jefe* stumbled home after long third shifts, he found his boys sleeping and snoring in the dark. The dirt from his boots tracked around the house and the kitchen for the boys to follow for years and years, as if their relationship were an investigation. *"These boys are all damn lazy,"* the *Jefe* says as he's called out by the *Jefita*. *"Get them out of my chair and to bed."*

"They've been waiting for you. Let them be."

This one morning, this one time, when the *Jefe*'s father, the *Abuelito* Ortiz, woke and sat in his nasty boxer shorts, reading his newspaper and listening to his AM radio, he poured Neto a tall glass of half-and-half along with a shot of Red Label.

"Drink this at every meal, boy," the *Abuelito* instructed. "And you'll be as your old man. Just like that." And when he said, "like that," he whistled through rotted teeth and snapped his fingers.

And when the man turned to fry morning eggs and bacon, little Neto climbed up onto his chair slowly and steadily. He found some height on the glass and balanced himself. He leaned into the table and down toward the glass, his tongue doing all of the work, lapping and lapping.

"What the hell is the matter with you, boy?"

Neto meowed and licked at his arms and his paws. Then at his neck and coat. He licked at his lips and hissed.

"I'm a cat, Papo." He continued at the milk, spilling white fluid over the table top and onto the floor. "So, I gotta drink like a cat."

The old man ripped the glass from the boy and paddled his bottom, slapped at Neto's face and chest. The liquid flew around the room and rained down on Neto's head. He made for his *Abuelita* and her soft attentive arms. The boy's face flushed red and tear-stained.

"What, are you giving the boy whiskey now?" Neto's *Abuelita* asked.

"A drink won't kill him."

And, in minutes, when the boy's *Jefe* and *Tio* Mitedio entered just through the back door, they both had words on the matter.

Tio Mitedio took off his hipster sunglasses and laid it out for the *Jefe*: "Relax, bro, he's just a little *moco*. The old man is nuts anyways."

Leaning against the wall the *Jefe* smoked and scratched at his chin. "It ain't right for a boy to act all sissy," he insisted. "That shit is for faggots."

"It don't mean nothing, bro."

"Mind your business. They're my Goddamn boys."

That night, as the family sat and ate in silence, the *Abuelito* cracked, "How's that pussy of yours, Santiago?"

In another photo I imagine 45s dropping down one after another. The *Jefe* turns the volume way up and the boys' dreams fill with the *Jefe's* music. Early on it was Clarence Carter and anything Stax and later Tejano, Little Joe and Al Hurricane. Records the *Jefe* heard out at the VFW. The *Jefita* doesn't dance or drink. "Ain't no way in hell I'm staying home to this, boys," the *Jefe* announced.

The music consumed those nights and early mornings to the dawn. The boys taught the woman steps, danced alongside their *Jefita* as she wept. They sang and cleaned cobwebs from the corners and from behind the sofa and along the *Jefita's* wooden floors and drapes. They swayed to those records until the *Jefita* had the idea to smash them.

"Take them, boys," she instructed.

"The *Jefe* tells us not to touch, Mama."

"Take them from their sleeves and stomp them. We'll show that *Jefe* of yours."

The boys jumped and jived as they crushed out any idea of the *Jefe's* music. Next, as a team, they tossed the player out onto the front stoop. They laughed and reveled until the *truckito's* engine hit the unpaved driveway and died.

That night the *Jefe* came inside with tears of frustration. His hands found the *Jefita's* cheeks, crushing the braids down the sides of her face. The family knows all the trouble that year was on account of those records.

Once, Neto saw a man with hotrod flames on his shaved skull and neck working the bumper cars at the Colorado State Fair and immediately begged his mother. He envisioned inked fire demons on his neck and shoulders. In his coloring books he chose the colors and drew in, colored arms and torsos with intricate patterns of gore and depth.

The *Jefita* gasped when she saw. "Get it out of your head, Neto. There are no tattoos for the little ones." She held him in her wide arms like a baby and he struggled. "You're just a little thing." Finally, she relented and released the boy. Told him he would have to wait until far after her death and burial. And his father's death, and possibly the death of most of the *Comadres*.

He reminded her of the *Jefe's* tattoos, dancing skeletons and the word "Mother" on his biceps along with his Army tats. He reminded her of *Compadre* Julian's and Mitedio's forearms with their Marine tattoos.

"Your *Jefe* was old already," she argued. "In the Army when he got those. And your father's ink itches at him anyhows, Neto. And the *Compadre* Julian is a damned fool. No woman would have him."

The boy asked, "What about Mitedio?"

"Mitedio? Your *Tio* was born with them."

That night, Neto disappeared into the bathroom with *Tio* Mitedio's pen knife. At first he just pulled himself onto the sink and in front of the medicine cabinet, got into the *Jefe's* shaving cream and then his cologne. He pretended to shave and scraped hair from his face. When satisfied with his skin and look, he drew and grated broad random arcs at his forearm until the tile and floor streaked with blood. It was an experimental gash that made the boy ache and wail for his Mama.

"There's a hell of a lot of blood here," the *Jefita* warned as she ran over the boy's forearm with the *strapajo*. "He needs stitching."

The *Jefe* asked, "What the hell was he doing in here?"

"Your tattoos, remember? He can't get it out of his head and now look." She wiped at the boy's tears. "It's okay, *Mihjio*."

"Oh, Christ."

"Is that all you have to say? He cut himself nearly to death with that damn blade. What the hell was Mitedio thinking giving this to him?"

"He asked for it."

"*Oy lo*. Asked for it. Neto, did you ask for this?" she said.

The boy nodded and giggled from his seat on the toilet.

"Ah, *Mujer*," the *Jefe* said. "A boy has to have some scars eventually, no?"

If his father had been home that one night, little Neto wouldn't have done what he did. If his father had been there any week-night instead of working graveyard shifts at his beloved CF&I Steel, or draining beers down at Donahue's with his *Compadre* Julian and the rest of his sad crew of working men.

If Neto hadn't wet the bed or if he hadn't dreamed *Cocos* and monsters as he often did in those early years. If he hadn't been so restless, he wouldn't have wanted to escape the *Jefe's* house as much as possible to explore and imagine.

"Your *Tio* was always restless," *Compadre* Julian always sells to me.

"Could never keep that boy in the house. No matter the time of day."

And if the *Jefita* hadn't sent him to bed early or if the cousins and the *Jefita*'s foster boys hadn't laughed and joked about his ears, the way they stuck out, then he wouldn't have done it. If the neighborhood boys in the alleyway hadn't threatened him with a knife, the rusty thing old man Hernandez used to carve dog food out of the cans. And if they hadn't joked about his sad hand-me-down t-shirts and the ripped pockets of his Chinos, and if he hadn't fought and been sent to bed without dinner to cry himself into an early sleep.

In little Neto's mind he imagined stabbings. In his dreams they ran it through him like the bulls of Julian's *vaquero* stories, his *Tio* Mitedio's Albuquerque bar stories or one of the hundreds of old serials the boys watched down at the Chief Theatre.

He blasted out of bed, after those sweat filled dreams. Up from the basement and finding his sneaks on the back kitchen floor near the old Frigidaire, the *Coco* and monsters be damned. Then he found leftover chicken and cold corn tortillas to fuel his ride. His bike on top of the mess in the garage not so easy to grab and then through the back gate to the flickering of street lamps so strange and inviting as to keep him riding up and down the alley.

All until he found the courage at 3 a.m. to peddle over to *Tio* Freddie's old house on Box Elder. The place that scared the other boys and the one they all dared him to enter.

"You'll never sleep in there, Neto," they said. "*Cocos* own that place and are waiting for babies like you."

The boy couldn't resist the trouble. That house near the traffic of the new interstate, where the men had abandoned the job of digging out the basement and boarding over smashed windows. The place the folks all said should be burned to the ground. The place whose lock he couldn't wait to trick, like his cousins always modeled.

From the street he endured all those barking dogs chained to their yards and watched the west end of the steel mill, with its smoke stacks and water towers. The boy dreamed, watching the lines of steelworkers' rides and their headlights snaking around parking lots. Watching and wanting so badly to be as his *Jefe* and those working men, out somewhere other than where he was stationed that eighth year of his life.

He also drove down there that night remembering those two *vagamundos* he'd found sleeping in the back of the abandoned house. It was months ago but he still wished he had talked to the men instead of ratting them out, still wished he would find them there again. He remembered how the Jefe kicked them out on their lazy asses.

"Where are you going, *disgraciados*?" he wanted to ask them. "What's going on all over? How can I have freedom like you?"

There were never enough answers for the boy. He put it to his Mama all the time: "Where do they come from?"

"No place in the world will keep men like those," the *Jefita* warned. "They have no place."

The words only made little Neto more curious about the neighborhood and that old house. That old "brick thing" on Box Elder, the living room littered with dog shit. That old monster folks tried to sell since *Tio* Freddie went off to sleep in the back bedroom and never woke.

Inside, the lights were all bare bulbs and the walls so thin you could hear night winds as well as mice nestling. And riding his bicycle indoors at night still gave him thrills, gave the boy a sense of risk he associated with steelworkers and hard travelling men.

If the neighborhood had been different for children in those days, he wouldn't have fallen. He wouldn't have been lost through the wooden floor where the men abandoned their work for their drinking and for their shifts at the steel mill. His weak arms and wrists breaking his fall.

The boy's feet kicked up dirt and dust and he screamed his mother's name and even for his brother Relles. He stared up through the hole in the second floor to the bare light bulbs fifteen feet above. The boy cried for hours, all alone with his thoughts until the early morning. He hollered and swelled his lungs. Through the pain he tried to make fists first with his left hand and then with his right. Around five thirty a.m. he caught the inner ears of steelworkers walking home to their rented beds and rooms after long third shifts.

"Jesus Christ," they said, peering down. "Just a little guy."

And days later as little Neto nodded off at the dinner table with both arms in casts, the other boys slapped at his cheeks and stole his tortillas. Stole his rice pudding.

"Goddamn laziness," the *Jefe* said.

"Relax. Think of your blood pressure," the *Jefita* answered. "It's the pills make him sleep."

"No, it is laziness and weakness." He turned as if talking to some other woman, some other family. "Goddamn boys have time to sleep during the day, they got time to work out in the yard. This ain't a hospital."

He paddled the boy and his hand became flushed with blood. Later he threw the boy out into the back yard in his underwear along with his dirtying casts.

"Now that's a sight," the *Jefe* said, spying through an open kitchen window. "Let him be thinking of his troubles out there."

In the last photo I study, the oldest boy Relles and Neto work the smoke-filled back rooms of the *Jefe*'s VFW Hall. They searched out beer and wine bottles behind trash cans and from atop cleared-out booths. Where no one could see, they poured the so-called empties into one bottle to create a mix of alcohol and spit. The music pounded from the jukebox and they drained their beer and wine concoctions, mouths pressed tightly around longnecks greedily stealing final sips.

Relles was the first to see the *Jefe* in little Neto's actions. "I'm gonna smack you upside down with them bottles if you can't share," Relles said.

In the late evening when the dance hall cleared out and the *Jefe* abandoned them with no friendly *Compadres* or folks around, they walked home. Relles puffed the *Jefe*'s old pipe, most of the tobacco burned up and hurting his lips and nostrils. In just a few years he would witness Neto sniff at glue and then later paint inside of paper sacks.

In between parked cars Neto will stare at the surface of the sky and the wall of stars. The boy's mind leaving his troubles to the side streets of the old neighborhood.

The *Compadres* say, "For Christ's sake, Manito. You can't blame their father for any of that. He did the best he could."

These are the tattered bits from the albums my *Abuelita* keeps in her closet behind the old typewriter and her hope chest filled with framed photographs of her *Abuelita* Valdez and her *Jefe* from San Luis. The folks demand them and for her to remember until she cries, "I don't want to see any of those old dead faces." Yet she pulls them out and slides them in-between cleared place settings and over coffee mug stains and asks, "Was I ever that Goddamn young?"

And there are faces no one remembers. Faces outside in the yard and around the alley. Maybe cousins or *Compadres'* children. Friends of the old *Viejitos* long since dead and buried. Foster boys with short lives in and around Spruce Street. "Maybe that is my Mama's cousin's boy from Chimayo," my *Abuelita* says.

"No," they say. "That is the boy they left when the mill shut down for good. They had too many kids to pay for. Don't you remember? You took them in."

"I have no idea who this boy in all these photos is," she repeats.

"See? That's why I don't want any of these damned albums. That's why I want them all burnt up. Burn them. All they do is remind me of what I can't seem to remember."

3. UNRELIABLE CROP

Neto drove us out to Vy Guzman's house near Taos Canyon. This was when he had the orange Nova with the bent frame and fucked-up transmission.

We were searching through her shed when the mustached Vy greeted us. She cycled a round through her shotgun. She laughed and pointed the barrel out to unpaved roads when she saw it was only us, flipped the safety. "For Christ's sake, Neto. I nearly killed your ass."

I was worried but Neto didn't miss a beat, dragged Vy's garden hose to cool the radiator and then saved the bleeding engine with some of her oil.

Vy said, "I thought you had yourself a truck, Neto?" She went over and pinched at me, ran her hands through my hair. "This Relles' boy? You Relles' boy? You look like him, no? You know that?"

Then Vy's obese and acne-scarred sister came alongside and wiped the lipstick from my cheek. Gave me a rough look. "No way. Looks like the mother."

The two took me around the house in through the back where they had a spread of fried Spam and eggs waiting. The room smelled of dogs and spoiled milk. Vy straightened the silver and turquoise belt around her skirt and then she stood on a chair in the doorway to re-place her gun. Vy said, scratching at her chin thoughtfully, "I expect your *Tio* every once and a while. Your *Tio's* not the kind to stay in one place. I see him every couple of seasons."

"Are you fucking kidding me?" the obese sister offered. "Like the *piñon* crop, you mean?"

"Yes, that's right. I say, if the *piñon* comes in for a bumper crop here in the valley I'll see Neto. I'll know he's coming for my tarps and step ladders. I know how he is. Every once and a while he meets women who don't understand. But I know."

"You make your excuses for him, Vy," the sister said. She smoked her cigarette and sat in her wicker chair alongside me, passed judgment with her eyes.

"That's just the way it is," Vy continued. She offered me the rest of the eggs.

The sister said, "You either follow him or you don't, *Hijo*. You hear me?"

"Sister!"

Then I sat with the dogs and while I watched some television, Neto and Vy giggled around in the bedroom, drained their rum and RC Cola.

"That Uncle of mines," Vy lectured over breakfast dishes, "reminds me of your *Tio*, Manito."

"Who?" the sister asked. She had her first cigarette of the day as she listened. "Manuel?"

"No. Ignacio."

"Ignacio?" the sister repeated. "He was loaded with money."

"I was thinking about this last night."

"Is that what you were doing in there last night. Thinking?"

"Sister!" Vy said. "The boy!"

"What?"

"Now hear me out," Vy said. "That old man was loaded, yes. That was for sure. And he used to bury his money in the backyard."

I drained my glass of milk and said, "My *Tio's* pockets are always empty."

"Yeah, well, that's not what reminds me of him. What reminds me of him is this one time he was out working."

"He was always out working," the sister said.

"Yeah. He was out working in the *campos* plowing. Near San Luis. He was a farmer in those days."

"Farming what?"

"*No sé.* Maybe lettuce. I don't know. What I'm trying to tell you is he was plowing and dropped the bank roll in the fields."

I asked, "Why did he keep it on him while he was working?"

"So the wife wouldn't get into it, Manito. Why else. Didn't want her getting the cash and getting out to town to buy groceries."

"Why wouldn't he want his wife to buy groceries?"

"You got a lot to learn about marriages, Manito," Vy explained. "Anyway, so he's out working hard and so he pulls his handkerchief, right? He pulls it and out drops the wallet and then he plowed right over it. So half the night he's out digging up the money and looking. He lost the whole family's bank roll because he didn't trust, you know?"

"What does this have to do with Neto?"

"Yeah," the sister added. "What in the hell does this all have to do with Neto?"

"Your *Tio* sleeping in there has never been that way. That's what I'm trying to say, I guess. Never hid money from nobody. Whatever he's got is yours. If Neto has money, then everyone has money."

"The problem is," the sister said, "Neto never has no money. And he ain't never going to marry you no how."

"Sister!"

Later as I climbed into Neto's Nova, Vy's sister handed me a black and white photo of my father. He was just high school aged, on horseback with Vy, who wore curlers in her hair.

"Oh, my," Vy said looking at the photo as if for the first time. "When you're young, *Mihijo*. When you're young things are so simple, no?"

"Then you grow up," Vy's sister said. They took turns kissing me. "Why do we have to grow up?"

Traffic zipped along the highway and soon my knees were in the dirt and I was collecting cones knocked from up high. Neto whooped and hollered as we moved from tree to tree. "Goddamn it, boy. We'll have hundreds of pounds in no time."

There were trucks parked with us: a Dodge with an old *Jefe* and *Jefita* that reminded me of the *Abuelitos* in Colorado; a woman by herself with just a truck filled with coffee cans and shovels; and two old men wearing warm coats and cowboy hats. Most were tourists and this wasn't their work.

"Manito," Neto instructed. "Watch that sap. Nothing will get that shit out so watch it. I ain't buying you no more pants."

I asked, "Is Vy your girlfriend, *Tio*?"

"What?"

"*Abuelita* says Vy's your girlfriend. Says you have a whole lot of girls. Says she broke up your marriage and the reason you sleep at Pete's. The reason you get jobs like this."

"That wife of mine was a snake, Manito."

"What?"

Neto made hissing noises. "A snake. You know?"

I looked at him dumbly.

"She hisses, Manito. Slides in an out of beds."

On the hood of the car we shared a lunch of bologna and Pepsi. I asked Neto if he and Vy screwed.

"Screwed! Jesus, Manito," he told me. "You get something in your head and you can't let it go." He pulled his Old Timer and cut the heart of a tomato, sliced it out with the long blade. He handed me a half. "Your *Abuelita* let you smoke?" Then he lit me a cigarette and handed it over. "That shut you up, no?"

After hours straining over sacks of *piñon* nuts, we finally pulled into a rest stop for the night. Neto sat on a picnic table and then smoked another cigarette and lit me another. He kept the headlights going.

"We'll roast these, Manito," Neto explained. "And then you know what will happen?"

"What?"

"We'll get paid."

I asked, "We gotta return all of Vy's tarps first, right?"

Neto threw his *vacha* out to the gravel parking lot and shot me a look. "Jesus Christ, Manito."

"You said you would."

"Where the hell did you get that?"

"I heard you promise, Neto."

For a minute Neto scrambled from his seat and then he drained the last thermos of water. "Goddammit, Manito. What in the hell is wrong with you?"

"She said you were unreliable."

"Who told you that?"

"Vy."

"Vy told you that?" He looked at the ground. His hands found his pockets and then he rubbed at his neck, walked in a near full circle kicking and cursing. "You'll understand someday. When you are a man. Vy has her sister and her parents. She gets a check from the state. Has land and a horse. We don't have any of that. You hear me? Do you see anybody leaving us land or money? No, Manito. Not like Vy's old man and her fat ass sister. Goddamn it."

"Ricardo gave you this piece of shit car."

"I fixed up this car. It *was* a piece of shit. Did you think of that?"

"No."

"You Goddamn right, boy. So I don't want to hear that. You say I'm shit and I say in your life, all you got is me."

"All I said was that the car was shit."

That's when he cracked me. Told me never to curse him. Told me my father was dead and rotting and that my mother didn't even want me. He just said it.

In a minute he jumped into the driver's seat, locked the passenger door and pretended not to hear me as I carried on. He fired her up and drove off. I lost my cigarette and cried until he put the Nova into reverse. I reached for the handle and he drove off again.

"Quit your crying," Neto said. He took a drag, and the dark smoke spilled from his nostrils. "A man doesn't have time for these games,

Manito."

The fatigue of the day's work rushed through me. My legs ached and my face stung hot. I ran off to the purple horizon and smelled the thick New Mexico night air, how it was distinguishable from all the other nights out with Neto. Neto's yelling cried above: "Goddammit, Manito! I'm all you got!"

4. CABRÓN

Sheriff Sheehan stood at my *Abuelita's* home on Spruce Street just after midnight and explained the whole sad situation. We were close, Sheehan and I. Must have run into trouble with him a dozen nights and each time the old woman took me in. That night she peered out toward the patrol car and mouthed the words, "Take him."

At the courthouse in Colorado City, I sat chained to a bench. A fat Anglo judge surprised me and met me personally, ordered me into an office.

"I'm McKensey," he said. He was short, wearing a gray sports coat and brown slacks, *whetto*-styled bolo tie. His hair was thin, combed-over a rather large and obvious bald spot.

"How long do I have to stay here?"

"Well let's talk about that." He took a pen from his dress shirt pocket and wrote without looking at me. He said, "Sheriff Sheehan tells me you are in a gang. Are you?"

"A gang?" My friends had walked down Northern Avenue and threw a brick through a passenger side window. I watched my brother Romes as he tricked the ignition with a long screwdriver. We tried to drive to New Mexico but only took that two-door Dodge and its little 4-cylinder engine past the abandoned dog track. We finally got stuck in a dune near the Chavez place, too dark to be exactly sure where. I was surprised Sheehan or anyone would think we were organized.

"From what I read here it looks like you should be in jail already," he said. "Does that sound right? And your Grandmother agreed that if it happened again you were going into the Youth Offender System. Isn't that what you all agreed to?"

"Yes, sir." My voice shook.

"I could put you in for six months." He put his pen down and rubbed his chubby chin with the palm of his hand. "Take you from your Grandmother. Is that what you want?"

The force of his voice made me flinch but I didn't say a word.

"Do you know what a miscreant is? Well, that's what you are becoming."

My throat started to tighten up, and I could feel the tears welling up in my eyes. He stopped for a minute, took off his glasses, and looked at me closely. "Do you know why you are not being arraigned? You know why you are in here? In my office?"

"No, sir."

"Your Grandmother. You know that? And because I know you lost your father and your grandfather passed, I'm not going to send you in. Nope. I'm not going to do it."

I stared at the pictures on his desk, his fat face and his wife and kids looking like fucking pros in their Sears catalog patterned shirts and smiles.

"If I give you six months, I don't think she could handle it. If you go it will change you. And I don't think that charming woman would survive such a thing," he said. He leaned way back in his chair. "You're heading down a path. That means prison. Once you're eighteen in this state and you steal a car your record begins. And we're not just talking about this place. This place is nothing. But we're talking Pueblo County Jail or Canyon City. Is that what you want?" he asked.

"No, sir," I said, speaking low.

"Well, all right then. That's what I want to hear. But you don't know how close you're coming. This is a dangerous game to be playing. And you can't win. Let me tell you, I know. You can't win. You'll never win."

My brother caught me walking behind the K-Mart. He was wearing a Dodger T-shirt hanging out over his khakis and had his cousin's purple Chevy idling. He had his hat to the side and the warm September sun was coming down on him. He looked hard. "I done it, Manito. Signed myself up."

"For what?"

"The Army, *Cabrón*. The Army." He had a cigarette in his mouth and every once in a while he'd blow smoke up in the air as he leaned against the Chevy. "I take the test and I'm on the bus in three months. You ain't gonna have me around no more."

His girl Armenda propped her legs out the open door and I caught a glance of her jean cut-offs scissored down close to her crotch. She was dark, tan and shimmering with lotion. It was nine a.m. and her eyes were already glazed from drinking.

I can remember seeing just three girls in my life who struck me as having that tough beauty. One was a thick Puerto Rican girl in the passenger seat of some *Compadre*'s Monte Carlo. She had a scar on her left cheek from a nail in her mother's couch after some guy fucked her. Her mother had trouble pulling her out the passenger-side window by her hair. This was the girl I would later marry. The second was a girl aboard a Greyhound on my way back from California to Colorado in 1999, who threw her soda can at her boyfriend who had just punched her. And the third was Romes' girl, Armenda Aguilar. Romes held jobs in Wyoming, New Mexico and even Kansas, but he always came back to this girl. He just couldn't stay away.

She stared with these big, green eyes. "Yeah, Manito. We need your gas money."

I lifted my pant leg and lowered my sock and showed them the ankle monitor.

"That don't mean nothing."

Romes and I weren't brothers by blood, but he lived with us for a while in the same house with my Uncle Neto, who was also generally known to be a *cabrón*. That's what my *Abuelito* had called us. No matter what we had going on *Abuelito* would predict its imminent failure. One time we had this Monte Carlo up on blocks trying to fix the exhaust system and *Abuelito* told us, "You'll never get that shit going, *Cabrón*." Or he'd say, "The hell you think you doing there, *Cabrónes?*" He just couldn't believe the state of the neighborhood's little men. To him Spruce Street was just one nest full of *cabrónes*. And when the old man finally passed, Romes ran off to work in the Kansas slaughterhouses and never said anything of it. I knew he hurt but he kept it all invisible.

"Are you coming or what, *Cabrón?*" Romes repeated. "Yes or no because I'm not waiting all day on you."

"Shit. I don't care." I stared at Armenda's dark legs. "I don't care."

On the way out of town we made a detour. Romes had us pull up to a broken-down duplex over on the west side.

"I'm going in for one thing and then I'm out," he said. "You want to come in?"

"No one's home?"

"That's why we're here," he told us.

It didn't seem odd that we climbed the porch with a pry bar and then he knocked. But he didn't knock again and after a full minute he smashed and kicked at the lock. Inside, our feet dirtied up the carpet and our footprints soon lay all over the place. Inside there was no furniture or frames on the wall. The rooms were all empty except for stained mattresses and soiled blankets.

We found the picture of Romes' father in a shoebox while tearing through clothes for dollar bills. The foster mother had tucked it between his birth certificate and some letters. It was the only picture

Romes had of his father as a young man, before he married his mother. From the looks of it somebody snapped him at a street party at his old east Denver apartment. In the photo, he is surrounded by laughing uncles and cousins Romes never met. We stared at it, all shiny from our sweat and our terrible feelings.

"Check it out," Armenda said. She was holding the dollar bills and the certificate. "Your name's different on here."

"That's not my name," Romes said. "It's my father's."

That afternoon on the highway was cloudless and the sky wide open with blues and turquoises. Along the roadside, the Union Pacific tracks rolled through hills and gullies, spread out from the highway out into peaceful rangeland. Sunlight came from the morning sky behind us, from above the Sangre De Cristo Mountains. We couldn't resist pulling over to see Huérfano Butte just south of town.

"You know they say it is really a volcano not quite formed." I stared out from the back seat. "Just the neck of one."

"Bullshit," Romes said.

Armenda said, "Maybe learn something if you'd just listen."

"Fuck you."

And then there was nothing, and we just parked and stared. Later I tried to get at him. "Don't you remember? *Abuelito* told us the Utes thought we all came from the mountain range here. You remember, Romes. He said men and women all just walked out from inside of her. Like it was heaven or God or something."

"You're so full of shit, Manito," Romes said. "The man was Catholic."

Armenda said, "Utes and Comanche were here before the Catholics. And the mountain and the red there, they strip mine with great big water hoses and then paint it all red."

"And nobody says anything?" I asked.

Romes said, "Shit. What you gonna do when you don't have me to drag your ass around no more? Who you gonna lecture?"

"You're not even listening." Armenda held her arms up on the headrest and her legs high up on the dash. "You'd learn something if you'd just listen. They're gonna love you in the Army."

"What the hell does that mean?" Romes had an unlit Camel in his lip and it bounced as he spoke.

"They're gonna kick the shit out of you, that's what it means."

"Jesus. You bitch."

"Just telling you."

"Shit, those pussies can't do nothing to me. What you say, Manito? You think we can handle 'em?" He looked over his shoulder and gave me a nod.

About twenty miles out of Huérfano County we hit a stretch of gas stations and a truck stop. We were thirty-eight miles from New Mexico, I could tell by the signs. Then Romes nosed in next to a pump and grabbed my ten dollars. He lit a Camel next to the pumps even though Armenda told him it was stupid.

"This is something you just don't get," my brother sang, "I don't give a fuck, I don't give a shit."

Armenda and I sat and watched a group of tanned kids wearing shorts and sunglasses, smiling around a mini-van. The folks behind the wheel I imagined as the mother and father. The van had California plates and the racks on top were full of luggage and camping gear.

Armenda asked, "You think those girls are pretty?"

"Which?

"You blind?" She pointed out the window and caught the groups' attention. They turned and stared. "You're as white as they are. Your dad *gabacho* or what?"

"He's dead."

She gave me a look of real horror. "Oh, shit."

"It's okay," I said. For a few minutes there were no more words between us. We both watched Romes pump the gas and then as he stood in line to pay.

Armenda finally asked, "How'd he do it?"

"Do what?"

"You know." She took her index finger and made like it was a knife cutting across her tatted neck.

"Crash site in his car. I was too young."

"Wish my old man was dead. Fucker would live through a hurricane and two heart attacks to rub up against me. The fuck."

I nodded my head.

"So I'm saying you're lucky. I think you're lucky," she said. Armenda drew up her hair into a ball at the back of her head and tied it all down with a band, exposing her brown neck.

I said, "They've got bigger chests than you."

"What?" She was half pissed and half laughing. "Who the fuck says 'chests'? You fucking with me, right? Better not be fucking with me."

"You asked me and I was just telling you."

"I asked you if you thought they were pretty. Not about their *tetas*." Then she pulled up her t-shirt, flashed me and the entire gas station.

"These are the real shit."

Around 1:30 Romes got pulled over. Armenda was the first one to catch the Trooper's lights in the rearview mirror.

Romes began to complain. "A hundred Goddamn rides out here on the highway and they gotta pull us over."

Armenda agreed. "Fucked up!"

In a minute we were standing on the shoulder as Trooper Barnes asked about expired tags. He went through the glove compartment and then under the back seat. He had us cuffed and kneeling with prayer out on the blacktop. It was only a matter of time before he found me out.

We stood and spoke carefully as the clear afternoon turned to a general grayness. Or maybe that was another time out on the highway. There were so many versions of this with Romes and Armenda, friends caught in moments that we thought hollowed out or helpless. I am not sure of the wrong or right of it. Plenty of opportunities in my bottom bunk of the Youth Offender System to sit and imagine. Each time I thought of Armenda as she made her finger cut across her neck.

5. DRIVEN TO THE FIELDS

The *Jefe*'s voice woke him. Over crumpled sheets, arching his sore back and sunburned arms over the mattress, he looked to the exposed bulb and to the open basement window. He could tell by the lowlight behind the window's coverings that it was still early, maybe before dawn. He lay on his back and let his thoughts come to him, let his body completely wake. He stared up at the unfinished ceiling and watched a spider crawl over its web in tiny steps, barely perceptible. He thought of how *Tio* Mitedio preached that to kill a spider in the house was bad luck.

A beam of sun finally came into the room and then the boy slid his legs out of the sheets when he heard the *Jefe*'s voice again:

"*Levantate, Cabrón*," the *Jefe* said. "There's time to sleep when we are all dead-meat and buried, so get your ass up."

The boy had avoided the *Jefe* all the previous day and night and found himself now in a place where he could no longer deny the father's authority. It was the days of summer break, and the *Jefita* was out to work and the *Jefe* was in command. He feared the man who he knew had the right to hit him if he wanted and would exercise that right. The thought, however, did not speed up or otherwise affect his performance on these long days of work.

This was the morning of the 4th of July and the boys looked forward to fireworks at the high school football field, barbeques and *pan dulce* down at *Tio* Freddie's. But that was before the *campos* and the work of *Jefe*'s side-jobs. Before *Tio* Freddie turned up dead. Those holidays seemed years past, even though it had only been one month since the *Jefe* decided eight-year-old little Neto, his brother Relles and the crew of fosters were to be taken to the fields, just one month since the *Jefe* called the boys "working men" and brought them out to Avondale, just outside of Blende, Colorado.

The previous year the *Jefe* had taken them to ball games and picnics and swimming parties at Bessemer Pool, the *Jefita* always by his side. But now the boys were driven to the onion fields for work to contribute to the family as men.

In the bathroom Neto pulled his work overalls and his cleanest, dirty white t-shirt. He washed his teeth and his face the way the *Jefita* had always instructed, and he looked for the notes she sometimes wrote for him. He looked for her in old clothes and laundry strewn on the floor and over the sides of the tub.

As he washed he smelled the air for coffee and bacon. He kept thinking of those dogs and *pan dulce* from last year's picnic, and he wondered if the day would lead them to a party with the *Tia's* baked enchiladas or her immense tables of summer goodies instead of boiled eggs, the warmed fried potatoes and refried beans he had grown used to. At breakfast he ate his cold tortilla, and he mumbled under his breath, "Don't want to go."

The *Jefe* heard and threatened the hand and then the belt. He instructed the boys to wash and dry the dishes, to pack the lunches and fill the thermoses with coffee and the mason jars with water. Neto rubbed the *Jefita's* lipstick from a coffee mug with a towel as he heard the truck's old engine fire and sputter to speed and then calm down. He wiped a plate when he heard the *Jefe* again yelling.

"Come on, Neto," Relles said from the backyard.

"Where are we going?"

"Where do you think, Neto? I have the front seat."

"I have to put my shoes!"

The boy tripped his way out to the truck, his shoelaces untied and the *Jefe* yelling: "Tie your shoes, *sonso*, or you'll break your Goddamn neck."

The *Jefe* held a large mug while he smoked and the dark smoke filled the cab. "And get that dog out of the back," the *Jefe* said. "I don't want to be watching for snakes all damn day."

The boy knew that no matter how often the old truck broke down, no matter how many flattened tires or miles of rain, nothing would stop the day's work from getting done. The crew would move and work until lunch and then only for an hour stop to eat before going back at it until just short of dinner. There would be only work, the dirt-kneed work of digging and cutting at the onions. The filling of baskets and then the filling of bags. The pungent odor and wet earth.

The road out to *Compadre* Julian's job was an unmarked trail off of Highway 50 past what they called Old Salt Creek. At the 39th1/2 lane towards the Fountain River and about a mile off of the highway and another mile off the pavement, the *Jefe's* truck hit the straight, unpaved lane out to Julian's piece of land. Along the way the boys watched horse and cattle settlements out past the Musso's farm, out past where the *Jefe* used to keep horses when he first moved from New Mexico.

As they passed, the *Jefe* wondered about the mud as the truck leapt and swayed; the boys in the back hunkered into the bumps and

Neto was airborne for a quick second before his backbone slammed down to metal truck bed. Relles held tightly to the lunches sitting next to his father and struggled to keep the paper sack filled with bologna and mason jars of water from slamming into the gear box.

The road softened and the tires spun. The rear end fishtailed. The *Jefe* compensated, but no matter his struggle with the steering, the truck slid off the road. Wet earth slid around bald tires and great walls of mud rose to each side of the tire wells and bathed Neto and the two fosters, covered the sacks and the wicker baskets. Neto's legs and sneaks struggled for traction and for balance. The boys nearly fell right from the bed.

As the truck bottomed out and found rock over on the shoulder, the *Jefe* hollered and yelped along with the boys. He slid open his door and slowly lit a cigarette. "How'd you like that one, Neto?"

The boys wiped mud from their faces and hair, from their coveralls. The boys screamed with joy, sat laughing and open mouthed as they wiped mud from their ears and eyes, their muddy hands and limbs marking over the rear panels. The *Jefe*'s head shook as he surveyed the truck, while the horses and cattle stared in wonder at the muddy crash site.

"In my day," the *Jefe* informed his crew, "they called it tank slapping. In the Army, I mean."

He stepped out into ten inches of mud and all the boys stepped out with him. He kicked and thrashed at the ground. Then he leaned down under the truck, inspecting. Each step sucked his boots into the mess as he waded from tire to tire until he found sturdy green grass and stable earth a few yards from the truck.

"*Ay que Cabrón,*" the *Jefe* said. The man cursed every bald tire of that old primer colored Dodge. He sucked on the *cigarillo*.

For long minutes he thought of walking the boys, of caravanning the whole crew out to Julian's tow chains. Then he thought of collecting wood to jam under the tires.

The *Jefe* chose rashly, chose to return behind the wheel of the rig. To let the *truckito* do all the work along with the crew of young boys. This produced more streams of mud to collect on the heads and clothes of the soaked Neto and crew.

"This is as far as we can go, Papa," Relles said.

Just then the boys and the *Jefe* heard a stream of water burst from the radiator cap. The steam cried from the cracks under the hood.

"Look, Papa," Relles said. Neto and the other fosters did not dare say a word.

The truck found its way deeper into a steep shoulder of mud and rock, rocks the crew of Neto and the fosters tried to kick loose and shove under the back tires.

He opened a mason jar of cool water and drained it with resignation. He smoked and cursed the day and the existence of onions. He cursed the *truckito* and kicked at the tires. He forced the hood up and attempted to grab at the radiator cap. He sat and waited for the rusty thing to cool. Meanwhile the anger had him.

"Goddamn it. I come out here with little boys and I need men," the *Jefe* cursed. He told the foster boys they weren't his sons, and he told Neto and Relles the fosters worked harder than his real boys.

He held Relles by the arm until the skin turned red, pushing the boy to move faster at collecting wood to shove down under bald tires.

When he finally cooled down, he tried the positive: "Goddamn it, boys. Get that wood in there. Get us the hell out of there. That's a way, boys."

The *Jefe* clapped and yelled up into the blue, late morning sky. He dragged Neto behind the wheel and gave the boy a quick lesson at the stick shift before digging in to push alongside Relles and the fosters.

"Let the clutch out and go as I say, Neto. You hear me? Go as I say?"

Relles said, "He won't be able to do it, *Jefe*."

"Shut it, boy."

Just then Neto fired up the *truckito* and rammed the shifter into first. His feet barely reached the controls yet somehow he found the gear and let the wheels spin as the transmission popped.

The *Jefe* pushed and strained until he had his pockets filled with earth and rock and his face covered in mud. He dirtied all his cigarettes, his pack and matches kept in his back pocket. The truck slipped out, finally fish-tailed onto the heavy grass. The boys' sneaks and pant-legs dug and slid deeper into the earth, and they watched the *truckito* jump and lurch.

Neto found second gear somehow from the clutch and his wild thrust of the stick shift. The boy had seen the *Jefe* groan through those old gears over a thousand runs to the fields or to the landfill. This time the boy had the wheel, and though his wet sneaks struggled to keep the gas and clutch down, he kept moving slowly.

The *Jefe* growled as he ran. He bowleggedly chased after, slapping at his knee and chest. He slipped down to one knee before breaking into a full out sprint. "Goddamn it," he wheezed under his breath.

The *truckito* rolled on and on, slowly picking up speed before winding down, stopping more than a hundred yards from the *Jefe* and the crew of boys.

When the *Jefe* finally caught up, he was red with sweat and mud. His boots were slick on the grass and dirt road. His fists clenched and tightened around a wet mass of cigarettes.

"Didn't you hear, Neto?" the *Jefe* said, ripping the key and killing the engine. He jerked the boy free from the driver's seat, Neto's knees dragging along floorboard and dirt road.

"I'm sorry, *Jefe*."

He slapped the boy with his wet hand, pushed the mush of ruined *cigarillos* into the boy's face and cheek. The *Jefe* had him by the collar, the coverall strap and then the arm. He slapped at the boy a second and then a third time.

"Don't do that, Neto. You hear me? You hear me?"

The wounded boy nodded and nearly giggled before crying, his face covered with a mush of tobacco, mud and snot.

"Don't ever go alone like that. You hear me, Neto?" the *Jefe* said, thumbing at the boy's chest and ribs. "Okay? Okay?"

"Yes, *Jefe*."

"Don't cry, Neto. The boys don't want to see you cry. No one wants to see you cry. Cut those damn tears out."

The *Jefe* searched for a smoke underneath the bench seat and then along the dash. Finally, he pulled himself inside and fired up the engine. He lit the cigarette and stared at the cracked windshield and then he backed up to collect the rest of the crew. Each boy looked soaked through and miserable in soggy coveralls. With little Neto up front, the *Jefe* steered on to Julian's side-job, the long day of work still ahead.

6. RETURN TO CACAVILLE

I met up with my brother Romes as I was leaving St Francis' Church. It was some sort of festival, and I was being dragged out to the parking lot by this kid Ando. I had arrived with my *Abuelita*, but it was other people who kept giving me drinks.

In between parked cars, we decided to slide into Ando's primer-colored Ford and kill time by visiting my *Tio* Neto out in New Mexico. Ando drove and Romes was passed out in the back. I strained over the bench seat, excited to talk. My brother was nineteen, and I hadn't seen him since he left for basic training.

This evening we drove out to the side of town they called Dog-patch, where not many people lived, and we bought something to smoke, enough we hoped to last about the whole trip. When we pulled up in front of a house, that's when Romes sat up with his thick, shaved head. Ando disappeared and returned with some nasty brick-packed shit. He kept nodding his head and smiling. "Can't believe I spent everything on this shit," he said.

"I need sleep," Romes announced from the back. Romes had always been more of a drunkard than me and Ando. Not so tall, but now after basic he was rail thin. He could order us around just with this deep voice, and I was envious. "How the fuck can I sleep when you *Cabrónes* are lighting up in the car?" We laughed and lit another blunt, giving a low light to the dark interior. I wondered out loud where we were going.

"I got a girl to meet," Romes said.

"Armenda?"

"Then don't ask me, *Cabrónes*."

The trip took us eight hours because Ando's junker threw a tire on the border of Colorado and New Mexico, just outside of Trinidad. Out on the highway, Ando kept pointing at the tire and repeating, "What the fuck do you know, Manito?" I watched an endless stream of eighteen wheelers and tourists heading north, the roar rising and then falling.

We passed an all-night Sinclair station around five a.m. and a faded sign marking the old highway down to Española and then to a small town called Dixon. The pavement ended four miles from a one lane bridge. Romes directed from the back. Take this left—take this road here—slow down—take this right. There were no real maps of this territory, and the trailer was not visible from any of the roads.

The morning was cold stillness, and the headlights of Ando's Ford lit up dust and weeds. The space around Neto's trailer was dirty with beer bottles and rusted machine parts. A gray dog was the only sign of life and the eyes looked silver and wolfish. Absolutely nothing happened when we honked the horn.

"This is the place," Romes said.

When Ando and I exited the vehicle, our eyes came across a cardboard sign up on the trailer. The sign read: Cacaville. Ando howled. "*Caca* is shit, right?"

My throat was full of sandpaper, but Ando was alive with energy, dying to meet Neto after all I had gone on about him. He shook his head and looked at me. "We made it, Manito."

Romes went around to the only un-curtained window and looked in. The trailer was aluminum, standing all by itself with two posts for a makeshift clothesline. The wild grass had grown around the wood planks acting as a doorstep. The apple trees gave the whole thing cover and nothing inside was clear to Romes, which made him look back towards us and slowly shake his head. My eyes were tired, and I wasn't sure if the grayish looking man who came to the screen door was Neto or some other sad soul.

He was smoking weed out of an old pipe and wearing old tan cowboy boots and a vest with no undershirt. His hair had grown out quite a bit and made him look rough. Mexican music blared from a small eight track player and he was silently mouthing the words.

"In a month of weird shit, man, you boys here at my door look about the weirdest," Neto announced. We all slapped hands. Neto gave me a sloppy, drunken hug that cracked my spine. "You're too damn skinny, *Cabrón*," he told me. "What does that *Abuelita* feed you?"

Inside the dimly lit trailer, we all got the full tour of a mattress and a small loveseat squared in front of a 19" inch television. Most of the places I knew my *Tio* Neto stayed were like this: one bedroom and a broken down bathroom the size of a closet, alongside a kitchen the size of a bathroom never with any running water or heat. The place smelled of bug spray and motor oil.

Then Neto invited us around a table for fried potatoes with onions and green *chile* he'd cooked on his camping stove. Neto even warmed tortillas and *posole*. He poured from a pot of coffee and added rum into the black liquid. "If you'd called ahead, I'd have made a cake, no?" He laughed and wheezed through his nose.

Neto looked wiry and grizzled at that time. He had tried to stay with my *Tia* for a while after a string of crash sites finally tore him down. I remember the day she had attacked him and thrown him out. She was behind me holding my shoulder and breathing hard; I imagined her tears were warm with anger and love.

He'd lost his work when the steel mill closed and his clothes were in a garbage bag; I think she even took the Bronco and the guitar. Later my *Tia* told me that Neto had refused AA and meds that would help his depression. She didn't know what else to do but let him go or murder him.

"I came to help you with your troubles," Romes explained during breakfast. "The Dodge, I mean. I hear you ran it into the ground, *Tio.*"

"You ain't got a car, Neto?" I asked.

Romes ignored me. "Ando knows more about cars than anyone. Thought he could help you with the job."

Ando nodded and smiled through a big spoonful of Neto's potatoes.

"My balls are too heavy to fix it." Neto grabbed at his crotch then he grabbed the handle of a green coffee mug and took a tremendous swig. He exchanged his pipe for a cigarette. "Need someone to do the work. Not help."

In minutes the work was settled. Romes would drive out to Española for his girl and for some drink, and he would try to cash some kind of check. Ando and I would get the Dodge running.

"Hey, *Tio*, you got a phone?" Romes was anxious to find the Armenda on her way from Culver City. He looked around wondering if this little spread of Neto's would live up to the promises he had made to her over the phone.

"No phone here," Neto said. He pointed out the door to his dog. The mangy thing was pawing at a dead mouse, not really knowing what to do with it. "Got one!" Neto screamed and then laughed.

"Come on, *Tio*. I need to make a call."

"Women are the death of you, and you don't mind dying, no?" The two slapped hands and out front Neto and Romes split the contents of a bag filled with weed or fungus. They passed each other dollar bills, and for a moment I fell asleep, right at the table.

Later, Neto handed me a can of gas, handed Ando two quarts of oil and a bucket full of rusted tools. My legs were stiff after sleeping on the cold table in Neto's trailer, and I had a hard time catching up to my *Tio.*

As we walked I pointed at the thin, white medicine strings on his wrists and elbows. "I'm getting old, Manito," he told me, thumbing at them. "Need help from the spirits out here." He gave me a look, reminding me that I had entered a place where people believed the devils that inhabited us could be seen. That you could bless them away. I suddenly remembered I was in New Mexico.

"*Brujo*?" Ando whispered to me and I nodded.

Soon we came to a grove of apple trees and a small clearing where Neto had built a makeshift foundation. He had placed a few boards out on the leveled earth, marking his plans for a small house in the middle of oblivion. It was about the size of two mini-vans, dry, and smelled like shit and burning garbage. Blackbirds were squawking.

Neto told us that he had been carrying some plywood and two-by-fours out in his old Dodge, and the engine decided to lock up. The propeller decided to just quit turning, and the whole assembly followed, leaving the truck in the center of the open field. It had lived there going on two months.

"I could have fixed her," Neto assured us. "But I was drunk and got the messages that flow the molecules from my brain to my fingertip receptors all discombobulated. It's all chemical and scientific, no? They teach you that in school?"

I watched as he staggered over and threw open the massive hood. He climbed up into the mess. He pulled a small screwdriver from his front coverall pocket as a doctor would, pointing out the complications to Ando as if on an X-ray. "What's happening in here seems to be the trouble."

Ando and I peered in and nodded our heads. "Needs oil," Ando told me. And then we began to experiment. We poured oil and put gas into the carburetor. Ando checked all the hoses. I got behind the huge steering wheel and tried to turn the motor over. First, the monster just coughed and clicked. Then oil wept through one of the rings and smoke started to slowly seep out into the morning air.

"She needs new plugs and a look at the wiring." Ando made quick work doing what he could and then he motioned to me. Again, it cried and coughed before finally exploding with intermittent, awful timing.

"Goddamn it," Neto howled at me through the cracked windshield.

"Ain't riding on all cylinders but she'll move," Ando said.

"This truck was my father's," Neto yelled through the windshield, which surprised me. "Your *Abuelito*. You know that?"

I shook my head.

By then Neto had the hood down and the tools in the back of the truck. He dropped into the passenger seat. "Let's get to town, *Cabrónes*. I'm still hungry."

I grinded through all the gears past Neto's planned house and then down a back way past his trailer. For a minute, after a long stretch of dirt road and mud, I thought the woods were going to crash through the windshield until we reached the old highway.

We drove and drove until we passed a stone handmade monument to *La Virgen de Guadalupe*. Neto had gone to some trouble to set it up out there in the middle of nothing, and he explained the merging of Christian and Mexican gods to us. Tried to educate us. Out in Colorado, Neto couldn't hold a job or keep a wife, but here in New Mexico, he was a keeper of old *brujado* secrets and knowledge, a real mystic.

A wannabe musician named Ronny from Kansas, this fat, lonesome girl Chalky, and Armenda, arm in arm with Romes, were all down beside me back at Neto's trailer. Under the New Mexican night sky, we sipped on cans of Bud Light and rum and RC Colas.

Ronny introduced himself as Armenda's cousin. Or maybe he said he was her brother, I can't be sure. But he looked older and rougher than all of us, except of course for Neto. He stood taller than hell and was a Cherokee, or at least that's what he told us. He went on and on about this slaughterhouse job in Kansas he worked at. "They give you a bloody smock and galoshes and a tin helmet and that's all the training."

As he kept on, I felt sicker and sicker.

"That's all. Then they send that shit at you and then the blood splashes you and splashes you and you can't keep up." He went like this for an hour, smacking his lips and gulping beer. "And then your arms go dead and you can't carry anything anymore and they still send them at you. Big fat bloody carcasses. And we eat that shit."

Romes just nodded in agreement. "Sickest shit you've ever seen."

My friend Ando mouthed the word "punk-ass."

"Tell your boy to chill the fuck out," Ronny told me. I noticed Ronny's head was narrow, and a silver safety pin pierced his left eyebrow. In a minute he rose up drunk and serenaded the campsite with some old tunes from his guitar. The beer made his chords and rhymes sound incomprehensible to me.

By nine that evening, Neto made an appearance and got a fire going. Half a case of Bud Light was gone. We had nothing to do but sit around and look at our drinks.

"Hey, Uncle Neto," Romes said.

"Yeah."

"You get scared out here? Out here in the middle of nowhere?"

"No. I got a lot of guns." Neto swigged from his beer and then put it down to answer. "Got one under the sink in there and under my bed." He struggled up to his feet from his lawn chair and moved past the campfire to his screen door. "Got one under my pillow," he said. "Got 'em everywhere." Ando just looked at me. Neto returned with a small, red handkerchief wrapped around a metal piece in his left hand, a fresh Bud Light in his right.

The piece turned out to be a clip-loaded job. I saw the gun under the red handkerchief probably before anyone else. He moved behind Romes and his girl to where Ronny had been playing guitar. He held the piece out into the deepest and darkest part of the foliage and quickly fired three rounds. Slam—slam—slam. His hand jerked violently and the empty cartridges flew straight up.

Armenda fell backwards.

Romes and Ronny both jumped. Chalky was probably the worst affected. She jumped and yelled, "If that man comes near me with that thing!"

I saw the rounds coming and I still jumped.

"What the fuck, Neto?" Romes cried. "Jesus Christ."

Neto wheezed and laughed. He continued to empty the seven rounds, but the last one sort of stuck in the chamber, and he had to pull at the metal cylinder.

In those few seconds of muzzle blasts, I had a vision of skull faces and drunken spirits surrounding Neto.

He looked at us. "Oh, come on," he said. "No one out here for miles and miles. It's St Ides heaven out here, Manito. St Ides Heaven!" He bellowed at the top of his lungs before going inside. I could see Chalky and Armenda squirming and not knowing if they should pack up.

The clouds didn't move that whole night after that, and in the dark I could barely make out both of the girls and their cut off jeans and t-shirts. They must have been freezing, but they were too drunk and stoked with cheap weed to care.

Chalky was the worst. She had jaundiced-looking scar tissue to her chin. I found out later that she was half-Indian like Ando, and that she was Armenda's half-sister. She wasn't as pretty as Armenda, her hair close cropped and mannish, which saddened her personality and demeanor.

I didn't want to talk but she sat so close. As my eyes adjusted she looked about twelve or thirteen.

"Who is that stupid old man?"

"Sometimes he's my uncle," I said.

"Sometimes?" She kissed me, and I could tell her eyes were outlined in black.

At daybreak I woke with that crazed feeling of being in an unknown place like I used to back in juvie. I'd felt like I hadn't slept but that I had just blinked my eyes. I didn't have my shoes or my shirt. Blackbirds were circling, and the shadows were gray in the darkness. I only had one of my *Tio*'s sleeping bags draped around me. I was wandering for a place to piss when I found Ando. Out in front of Neto's trailer he held his leg tenderly where a small, black hole had formed in the meaty part of his thigh, about the size of a cigarette lighter burn. Blood had formed a muddy black puddle on his jeans and on the ground around him.

"Sorry ass queer stabbed me," he kept repeating over and over. "Fuckin queer stabbed me!"

He pointed at Ronny who was sitting at arms-length across from him. Ronny looked white and sick, holding his own bloody mess across his face. His flannel shirt was untucked out over his pants, his long hair that had been tied behind his head had come loose, and he had lost what looked like a mouthful of teeth. He spat blood out onto his chest and legs. His guitar had imploded.

"Well," I said, looking to Ando. "Pull it out."

"Do you see the knife in me, *Cabrón*? Do you see a blade anywhere? Jesus, Manito."

I looked over the campsite at the empty bottles standing around at attention and couldn't scan the blade anywhere.

"The sticker didn't even get in there that far," Ronny said. He was digging through his shirt pocket for cigarettes.

I have half a recollection of what went on while I slept that night, more of a dream, really. Allegedly, my brother Romes kicked his girl Armenda in the stomach while they were sharing a sleeping bag. I'm not sure if they were fucking or fighting. I am not sure if it happened because Romes was drunk or because my brother was just mean as hell. Could've been either. Maybe he was like me and woke up not knowing where he was and freaked. I couldn't testify to any of this.

Suddenly and stupidly, Ronny walked right over with a knife. Somehow he managed to run it through Ando's leg. The sticker went right in and broke off; that would come to light later. Then my brother Romes and Ando reacted with a self-destructive move like we were all known for. They kicked and elbowed the hell out of Ronny, tearing at his legs and his chest while he fell. Armenda just lay there on the ground crying and begging.

Romes had staggered around looking for his girl's forgiveness. But not much later, she would get in Ronny's Mazda and roll out of sight of Romes' pleading face, deserting the sister and the bleeding Ronny into my stunted care. All I know for sure is when I got up the whole mess was done, and the wind was crying through the campsite.

What I am sure about was the long, winding drive out to the hospital. In the Ford were Ando, Ronny, the thirteen-year-old girl named Chalky and me; I was driving. Ando had the hood up on his sweat shirt; he bled over the seats and the floorboard. He cried over his wound, and it shocked me. Once, Ando had gotten into it with some kids in juvie who had tried to push his shit in. I remember Ando got his head bashed and didn't make so much as a grunt. He just punched and crumpled one kid down to the floor.

"Are you all right?" I asked Ando.

"What the fuck do you think?"

Neto gave me directions. I don't know how I found the hospital in Española. We sat in the waiting room and watched a television chained to the wall. Chalky wrapped herself in a blanket and sipped from a can of RC Cola. She had a look of not knowing what next. I wanted to put my hand on her shoulder or say words to console her.

"I never kissed anyone."

"What'd you say?" she asked me. "What'd you just say to me?"

By then it was noon, and we hadn't moved. I needed something, and the girl had cigarettes. She kept counting them nervously with her fat hands. She pointed out the burn marks on my fingers and the yellow nails from smoking too much. I noticed the dried skin on her arms and elbows. "Your *Tio* really live out there?" she finally asked.

7. LITTLE BLUE BOX

That summer little Relles thought the whole neighborhood heard his *Jefita* calling for him. The *Jefita* stood restless, frying *calabacitas* with corn for the *Jefe*'s lunch. Everyone heard her yelling for Relles through the screen door, screaming for him to run over to Joe's Grocery for her "little blue box." He only half-understood why she had him down there so early on a Saturday morning.

"Relles," she yelled before handing them the money. "Don't go to Marshall's, *Hijo*. Go to Joe's. Are you listening?"

"Yes, Mama."

"Then look at me when I'm talking at you, boy. Do as your Mama says and get going."

The crew of boys walked almost everywhere in those days, especially when the *Jefe* and the *Jefita* took their "naps." On those Saturday and Sunday afternoons when they forced the boys out for chores or errands, the *Jefe* gave the boys money and practically pushed them out of the yard. Most of the time they went to Joe's or sometimes during the week to Marshall's.

"It's because she's opening up and bleeding," the cousin Tevo revealed to Relles over the blocks to the corner of Summit and Box Elder.

"Shut up, Tevo," Relles answered. "Go back home."

When the boys arrived at Joe's, the place was just opening and Joe Appleguese was stocking his shelves. The place was a tiny living room converted into two small aisles of food and toiletries. All Relles had to say was "little blue box" and the man had his brown butcher paper out. He cut the paper with a long stationary blade on the makeshift counter and wrapped the box, sealing the package with tape. "Why don't your brothers ever come in?" Joe asked. He was wearing his coveralls and his apron made him seem official even if the place was a broken down and converted home.

"Those aren't my brothers," Relles said.

Back on the street Tevo kept on, "She puts them down in between her legs and keeps herself dry, *Cabrón*."

"Shut up, Tevo," Relles said. "I'm trying to count the money."

Neto had the most questions. "What's a blue box, Relles?" he asked. "Why does she put them down between her legs?"

"Shut up, Neto," Relles answered.

"No, I want to know," Neto said.

"A woman bleeds because she's got pains," Tevo continued with the lesson. "She flushes her eggs out once a month and bleeds. Give me the box and I'll show you."

"What eggs? Flushes 'em where? Down the toilet?" Neto asked.

Tevo said, "The boy needs to learn about things."

"That's enough. I don't want to know about the *Jefita*'s eggs or her bleeding. Now shut up or I'll tell the *Jefe*," Relles said.

"You shoulda went to Marshall's but the *Jefe* don't want you there."

"Why don't the *Jefe* want us at Marshall's, Relles?" Neto asked.

"Because the *Jefe* don't like the *negros*," Tevo answered. "Not as much as Relles anyhow."

"Shut up, Tevo."

"What? You never do nothing, Relles. Everybody on the block knows the *Jefe* don't like those *negros* or that store. I remember him asking you how you could eat those burgers from down there at Marshall's."

"What's wrong with them, Relles?" Neto asked.

"Nothing, Neto."

Tevo wouldn't give it a rest. "That old man Marshall and his wife are dirty and keep that place dirty."

"Old man Marshall was a war hero and your old man never even went into the Army," Relles said.

And with that Tevo snatched the wrapped box from Relles' arms and had the butcher paper ripped. Relles was mad but then curious. After all these trips for the *Jefita*, he had never opened or even peeked at the box. Never even thought of it until Tevo.

"Come on, Tevo!" Relles shrieked. "Give it!" The boys wrestled around in the dust and grass of Tommy Aguilar's empty lot. The crew giggled at first and then just watched as the two boys scraped and scratched into a gully and then into the back fence. They punched and kicked until the ground slapped Tevo on the side of his face.

The butcher paper tore into shreds and then the blue box with the letters spelling out "Kotex" got crushed beneath the boys. What looked like rolled bandages fell out onto the dirt; one was crushed during the tussle and one unrolled. Neto inspected it. It got more attention from the boys than the *chingazos*. Neto held the pad in his fingers and marveled at the length and weight of it. The crew of boys just stared.

"Holy shit," Tevo said, running and laughing with the dirtied pad.

"Her snatch must be broken down because of all the boys she's pushed through."

"Shut up, Tevo," Relles said, wanting to end it. He thought of how he was responsible for the box and how the *Jefita* would be angered. Tevo was new and didn't know the house rules. Tevo hadn't once caught a beating. Not once had Tevo witnessed the other boys' beatings and that made Relles feel sorry for him, made him understand why the boy would act such a fool.

"Give it here, Tevo," Relles pleaded. This was nothing more than weakness to Tevo. That was when Relles tackled Tevo from behind and the two boys tumbled into the alley. The dust and the dirt flew around until Tevo revealed his bleeding face. His bleeding forehead caught a board and nail. The blood turned brown and the boy kept feeling at his head and temple searching for the blood.

"God, Relles," Tevo cried. "I'm only playing with you."

Relles grabbed the unrolled Kotex and replaced it back into the box. Then he marched back to Neto and the crew of fosters for the second lost one. His face glowed red and he breathed hard. "I told you not to mess with me."

"Fuck you, Relles, and your *putita* mother!"

"The hell happened here? The rest of you get outside and wait for your *Jefe*. Come here, Relles. Damn it," the *Jefita* said, first lighting a cigarette. "I give you one job and you can't even do that. I can't even count on you to do one thing for me *porque chingando*."

"I'm sorry, *Jefita*."

"*Oy lo*! Sorry?" she screamed. "What happened?"

"I dropped it, Mama."

"Come here, Relles. I want you right here. Your father relies on you when he's gone and so do I."

The boy dug the change from his pocket and dropped it to the table.

"Get over here," she said. Then the *Jefita* slapped Relles. Tevo and the rest of the crew and even little Neto laughed from the back porch. "And quit your crying," the *Jefita* said, puffing at her cigarette. The muscles in her jaw moved. "I'll give you something to cry about."

"Come here," she said. She sat down at the table and then she kissed the boy's forehead. She pushed his hair aside. "Your *Jefe* comes and goes. And your brother is all over the place. You're the man when the *Jefe*'s gone. You hear me, boy? You hear me? I rely on you."

Relles asked, "Are you bleeding, Mama?"

"Who told you that?"

"Nobody."

"These are for women."

"Yes, Mama."

"You don't need to know no more."

That night the rain fell down earlier than expected and all through the house there was no sound. Down in the basement the other boys slept undisturbed, and Relles sat on the back porch in silence, staring out over the patterns in the grass and the back fence that led to the alleyway. He thought of the windows and how he might climb out through the screens of the enclosed porch and then he cried, not entirely from his mother's hand, when the *Jefita* finally called for him to return to his bed and place alongside his brothers.

8. GROWN-ASS MEN

Neto searches for liquor store neon lights. Down Colfax past the Lebanese delis, the taco stands and hamburger joints. He shows me all the old Denver haunts and curses his primer-colored Chevy, an ancient, sickly thing, broke down with the hood up at red lights. He steps into the intersection and agonizes over her. "I tell you when you got nothing else she will leave you."

I say, "This car is delicate, *Tio*."

"Fuck delicate."

It takes us two hours pushing and waiting on some friend to get the ride moving again. We are puffing the whole way and by the time we are in bed we are both drunk and dead tired. Neto's still cursing over the breakdown while I'm waiting for a phone call from a girl I'm in love with.

Around midnight I hear the phone ringing and Neto laughs. He never likes the girls I talk to. He advises, "Don't fool yourself, Manito. These *putitas* are dangerous and you don't know *porque* you're still young. But I know."

I remind him he isn't my father. I tell him to go to sleep.

Trina's voice sounds tired and breathy. She says, "I've been wanting to talk."

I hate her for not calling me and not coming around, for fucking Arthur Sandoval and never lying to me about it. I keep it inside, put myself down on the couch and click on the television. "I was about to go to sleep."

I can hear her peeling off her uniform. I imagine she smells of grease and cigarette smoke from her airport diner gig. Then I imagine her naked. I ask, "How's things? Haven't heard from you in a while."

"Talk to me until I fall asleep, Manito," she says.

"Why do you call me?"

"Do you want to talk to me or what? Be my friend."

That night Trina spits out the worst thoughts about her father and about her shit-jobs, convinces me Sandoval's brothers burned her with a cigarette and stole dollar bills from her purse. She speaks seductively and gets me worked up and then she falls on to sleep. Towards dawn, all the sounds of the trailer park calm down and it's just me and her breathing.

It's raining and Neto and I hit traffic at the bus stop, across the street from his trailer. We're walking, though, heading out to find some food and coffee.

Neto says he heard me last night, taunts me about it the whole time. "I'm surprised she hasn't gotten you to do her laundry, Manito."

"Shut up, Neto."

Four blocks go by and then farther down East Colfax toward Lakewood we catch a ride downtown to Larimer from one of Neto's *Compadres*. I leave Neto for more walking out to where this girl I know works counter service.

Inside I ask for food. Ask her about her old man. The one who threatened me one night coming from her bedroom.

She says, "He's in the Gulf."

"Where?"

"The War."

"Oh," I say.

"There's no food here for you. I ain't gonna lose my job. I ain't your girl."

Neto is in line and has his wallet in his hand. In the heat he removes his shirt.

She asks, "Is that your *Tio*?"

"Just some corny guy. Just some dude."

"Hey, Manito," Neto says. "You want a coffee? I got enough for a coffee."

Later that afternoon I call the counter-girl for about the tenth time from a pay phone at the VA over on Colorado Boulevard. Neto has an appointment and I follow him down there. I'm always following. I wait until Neto goes in to see the doctor and the line rings and rings.

Trina calls me again and tells me she's reading.

"What the hell is in those books?" I ask.

"Don't hate. Never saw you read in school much anyways."

"Not much time, you know. I got this going on and I got that going on, you know. I'm full of ideas."

"Fucking liar."

"I got ideas," I say.

"Well, these books have ideas in them, *Cabrón*. Did you know the Catholic Church said Mary rose into Heaven. It's not in the Bible but a Pope said it's true. Pius the 12th."

"Whoa, you know your Popes," I say. "Your father teach you that shit?"

That night she talks dirty to me and then she comes over after Neto is out. She has a friend drive her. First we watch some videos Neto has on Vietnam and I tell her about my old man being in the war. She fucks me right on Neto's couch in front of the TV. I feel the bruises on her body, her arms and thighs.

Trina's father has one arm. He wears one of those clasping hooks. I've seen him come in pretty regular to the diner where she works. He works maintenance for one of the airlines out at Stapleton and comes in for a lunch of a sandwich and a soda. I'm there three times in a row before Trina introduces me.

He's a vet of the Ordnance Corps like Neto, but he works 40 and sometimes 50 hours a week. He works a second job at one of the department stores downtown. They live off of West Colfax; me and Neto are east.

I tell Neto about the arm.

Neto asks, "Did he lose it in the war?"

"He lost it in the steel mill, I think."

"Ask him," Neto presses.

"I haven't met him."

"Meet him, Manito. A man's got to meet his love's father."

"She ain't my love."

Trina's father shakes my hand with his left. His shirt covers the arm, tied off with a safety pin. I stare at it a few times right when he is talking to me. I thought he'd have the hook.

"Trina says you don't work?"

"No, sir," I say. "I'm in college."

"She's going to Denver University."

I nod.

"She has to earn money," he says. "Anybody who wants work can find work."

I nod slower.

"I went to the community college in Colorado Springs," he says.

"How'd you lose the arm, sir?"

Trina is watching from her register, and as she rings up this lady's coffee and sandwich she gives me a look.

He says, "I lost it working."

"I mean how'd you lose it? Cut off or smashed? Stuck in a machine?" I say. "A friend of my *Abuelito* lost his ear in a blast furnace. Burned right off. He could still hear he just didn't have the meat, you know."

The father walks from me, back to his shift.

I say under my breath, "He grew his hair long and covered it up. He was always embarrassed. Just embarrassed, you know. Didn't want no one to know about it. Edgar Sais. That was his name. Didn't want nobody to know."

In a minute Trina tells me how stupid that is. Tells me how stupid I am.

"Why do you do such *cabrón* things, Manito?" she asks. "I can't even trust you to talk. No one talks to the old man like that."

The next chance I have to meet the father is over dinner. We all eat strawberry pie for dessert and the man asks me questions about my family, my mother and father.

"Your grandparents raised you?" the father says.

"Yes, sir."

"Where were your parents?"

"They just weren't around," I say.

"Well, where were they?"

"Leave the boy alone, *Viejo*," the wife says.

"He's doing fine."

I finally say, "My father died and my mother lived in California while I was growing up."

"That's odd. Don't you think that's odd?"

"*Viejo!*" the mother cries.

"I just think that's odd," the father says.

"Leave the boy alone."

Then I pull my cigarettes and smoke right there at the table. I don't go out to the porch like the girlfriend wants and instructed me to. I just sit right there at the table and take long drags and don't say another word. I smoke one after another leaving *vachas* on the table and putting them out in the leftovers of my plate.

Later she tells me not to call her but I do call her. I call her about every day. I call her at night when I think the old guy might be sleeping. At work and at her grandmother's. I call just about everywhere I think she might be.

One time I have a conversation with her Aunt. This is weeks later when I hear Trina is dating some *whetto* from Littleton.

While Neto's out I'm on the phone talking to the old woman about unhappy lives and dead-end jobs, and this woman has no idea what I'm talking about.

I hear a voice in the background. It sounds like a woman's voice. The voice tells the Aunt to get off the phone, tells the voice Trina says I'm a psycho and then the lady hangs up on me. The line goes dead and I call back again. Finally a male voice answers, tells me to quit calling and that he knows who I am and knows where I'm living. The voice says they knew who my *Tio* is. Says they know my people and how I am.

Days later I finally get Trina on the phone. She picks up one day at work. I'm in my underwear sitting in front of Neto's television watching Vietnam videos. Trina's weeks from heading to college.

"You're a liar. You told my old man you're in college. You ain't in college. You didn't even finish high school."

"I'm getting my GED."

"Quit calling and coming around."

I say, "I haven't been coming around."

"You didn't drive by my Grandparents' and flash your headlights?"

"I didn't do that."

"Well, you the only fool I know who drives a fucked-up Chevy. Don't call me. Am I the first girl you ever dated or what?"

"You can't just abandon me."

She's quick to laugh: "Abandon? You do that with children and not grown-ass men, Manito."

That night after the *Tio* passes out I stare at Neto's trailer, the sty of a kitchen and the bathroom the size of a closet. The closet the size of a cabinet. I stare so hard my eyes ache. That whole summer I sit in Neto's life.

9. *JEFITA'S* DRESS

Near the alley where Relles, Neto, and the crew of fosters went crazy in the gravel and sea of rusted machine parts that was their playground, the *Jefita* waited in the kitchen. She organized her shelves and her drawers, seasoned old cast iron skillets to pass time; she mended holes in socks and in the knees of the kids' clothes, crocheted blankets and sewed full-length dresses she never wore.

"Where would I wear them?" she said as much to herself as to the boys when they entered. "I can see myself wearing them to the cleaners as I'm pressing clothes. Maybe I'll wear them out to the onion fields. Your *Jefe* would love that, no?"

One time she worked while the boys watched cartoons and conducted wrestling contests. First she found a community of fire ants living under the sink as she completed the breakfast dishes. Then she peeked down at a drowned mouse inside of the wash basin. She screamed twice while the boys laughed and while the *Jefe* rested to drain his rum and RC Cola.

She convinced herself the ants bit up her legs and mice gnawed all of their underwear. She imagined diseases and illnesses spreading through the household.

"*Cabrónes*," she yelled. "We could drown in filth and you wouldn't even lift a finger."

The boys and the *Jefe* rolled with laughter and then howled as she ran around, smashing and slapping with the broom. "Clean this house," she said. "Do something for Christ's sake."

At first the boys laughed, but they were frightened when the *Jefe* went over to the woman and yelled. He waved his hand, dismissing the wife's concerns. "Keep up your Goddamn screaming," the *Jefe* said. "Your screams will scare the bugs away. I won't have to do nothing, *Mujer*."

"Why the hell don't you help me around here?" the *Jefita* asked.

Relles was the only boy still laughing as she began to cry.

"No, *Jefe*," Relles said. "Screaming don't kill bugs."

"You boys have no more sense than your old lady. I'm surrounded by little girls instead of men," the *Jefe* said. "I got side-jobs today."

"Side-jobs. Side-jobs. All I hear is your side-jobs," the *Jefita* said.

"You're a Goddamm ungrateful bitch of a woman just like *su* Mama. Where would you be without the money me and your boys bring in? The mortgage don't pay itself. We produce."

"And where would you be without my cooking filling your fat belly and my cleaning of your stinking shorts, *Viejo*?"

"Mama," the fosters said.

"Shut up, boys," the *Jefe* yelled as he pushed and dragged his wife by the forearm and then the hair in a frightening dance.

"I never meant to marry such a no good bastard as you."

"Well I got news for you, *Mujer*. Your Goddamm food ain't that good no how." And as he slapped her face the house went dead quiet. No television or laughter. No boys crying or calling for their mama. Later as the *Jefita* walked the backyard to smoke her cigarettes and stared up into cloud-infested skies, she thought back to her father's words about the *Jefe* and his kind.

In the dark Santiago and Cordelia were whispering. They slipped into the back seat of Santiago's 48 Packard. So many of Cordelia's sisters met men and left the family ranch in San Luis. It seemed beautiful to love a man.

"Oh, Cordelia," Santiago said. "You are so Goddamned fine."

She giggled and rolled into his arms. She had danced down at the VFW with so many men until she chose Santiago because he was a man in uniform and a man with work and money. He was a man with the goal of trade school and a man with work in the steel mill miles north.

"Do you love me, Santiago?" she said. "Or do you just want what's between my legs?"

He gripped her closer and then kissed her softly down her perfumed neck and shoulders. He knew why he drove these empty back roads.

"Be careful," she said that night.

Santiago pressed his large frame over Cordelia's until she struggled and then accepted the drunken man.

Months later, doctor bills, and then a baby wrapped in one of her knitted blankets and held close to her young breast.

"Is he dead?" Santiago asked over the bench seat. "I don't hear no crying so he must be dead, no?"

"He's fine," she said.

They drove until the driveway of the mortgaged home, blocks from the steel mill and hundreds of miles from Cordelia's family home.

At the first sunrise alone with her son, she wiped at her tears and then shook Santiago awake. Her Santiago slept through the alarm clock and then through her words and shakes. He was late for his day shift.

"What in the hell happened?" the *Jefe* said. "What good are you if you can't wake me, *Cabróna*? I have work. Can't you see? Don't you know work or did your old man have you that Goddamned spoiled?"

"I know work," she returned.

The *Jefita* walked to the bus stop thinking of schedules and routes, and later she observed road and brick buildings through glass windows as she rode. She became dizzy at the downtown depot because of squealing brakes and honking horns. Inside the depot the *Jefita* drained coffee and considered the highway. She rested near ordinary couples spooning soup and handling sandwiches, kissing loved ones and making sweet goodbyes. She covered her raw bruises.

And when the falling sun finally gave stillness to evening, the *Jefita* surrendered and stretched her sweater over exposed shoulders. She threw herself into the waiting *truckito*, slammed the metal door and rested her elbow to the passenger side window while the *Jefe*'s old engine fired up.

"A few Goddamn ants and you ready to abandon the whole house," the *Jefe* said. "Why the hell are you always doing this? You never gonna have the guts to get on."

"I might."

"Get it out of your head, *Mujer*. One day I won't come looking."

"One day I won't get in your *pinche truckito*," the *Jefita* said.

"Mama," little Neto said. "Why did you leave with a suitcase, Mama?"

She kept her eyes closed and she barely took the questions as each boy began to plead.

"You see, *Hijos*," the *Jefe* said. "One little thing and there she goes getting mad and leaving you right away."

The *Jefita* sat weakly as her *Jefe* lectured. Beneath the primer colored *truckito*, out over the 4th Street Bridge, Union Pacific train whistles sang to the *Jefita*.

10. PENANCE

When the pregnant girl dropped in the car, pushed in the lighter and finally lit her Kool, I had no reason to believe anything on the Chevy's dash to be in working order. I asked her, "Can't be good for the baby?"

"What?" she said. She was chewing gum, and she cradled her cigarette above her head. "The fuck put me out so I got to walk."

After the first ten blocks, out past Union Avenue, I still had no clue where we were headed.

"This is one of Luis' rides," she said.

"I bought it."

"He's been working on it."

"Don't worry. I'm takin' care of it," I said. On the bench seat, our bodies sat close, and we might as well have been holding one another.

"Where's he been?" Her feet kicked loose of white Keds, pushing them up against the book bag.

"New Mexico."

She laughed at my haircut, my excuse for a short sleeved shirt and tie. "Hey, you work at a bank or something?"

"A bank? What do you mean?"

"The tie."

"No, I got an interview," I told her. "I gotta wear a tie."

"Oh. Looks like you work in a bank someplace," she said. "You sure you're not in a bank someplace?"

"No," I told her.

We drove for a long time, until we reached her *Abuelita*'s on the east side of town. The house was sandwiched between a sectional home and the entrance to a littered alley. One dead-looking tree was planted out in front with a primer-colored '87 Ford Tempo parked underneath.

"I thought about chasing the fuck," she explained. She stepped out of the lowered car onto her street. "I thought about it."

I studied the way she lit another cigarette, watching her lips while she spoke.

"Always talked about Denver, jobs out there and shit, but nothing ever real, you know. My *Abuelita* says he has to marry me. Has to prove our love in front of God."

I couldn't think of anything to say to this. She was on her second cigarette. The light of late afternoon was shifting and a sudden dizziness hit me.

"You got a lot of tattoos," the pregnant girl said. "They hurt you?"

"Sometimes they ache." I lifted up my forearms as evidence.

"No, when you got 'em," she said. "When they were needling you."

"I was in the Army at the time and drinking."

"You can't get a tattoo when you're drunk."

"I was drinking," I told her. "I wasn't drunk."

"Oh, you don't remember the pain though, uh?"

"It was a mistake," I told her.

She nodded. "I got a small one." She slipped the straps to her jean dress and her bra down over her left shoulder, revealing a small set of initials. It looked like a prison tattoo, thick and blue.

"His initials?" I asked her.

"Of course. But, you know, BS. Like bullshit, right?" She leaned her head deeper and looked over her shoulder, pushing her red-streaked hair out of the way. "Jesus himself can see it."

"You didn't even say your name yet," I finally said.

A dog was barking down the block and I was just about to pop the column shifter into drive when she slammed my passenger door. "Angie."

The small house consisted of the *Abuelita*'s bedroom and bathroom off of a small kitchenette. The room was filled with crucifixes and statues. A banner measuring three feet across hung in the living room, just above the television and, intimidating as hell. "*Estandarte*," Angie explained me. "It used to be my *Abuelo's*." I got a better look at it as Angie and the *Abuelita* conjured sweet smells in the kitchen. A sculpture, ornate and made of wood, took up what was left of the living room. A deep, red, decorated Jesus with a thin frame and crowned head. His face sorrowful and hurt. A crack ran down his face opening wider around his chest, an imperfection in the wood. The sculpture looked as if it might jump, at any moment, to judge the living and the dead and focus in on me.

But the *Abuelita* took a liking to me right away. She was hunched over an aluminum walker and paced around the kitchen, complaining about what a shabby job Angie had done cleaning the sink and counter. Her voice rang in Spanish and climbed an octave as she explained the proper way for her plates to be stacked in the cupboards. When Angie introduced me as a friend of Luis', I watched the old woman, gauging her reaction.

"Name?" she asked. "Quick, boy. What's your name?" She communicated in a senile mix of English and Spanish, mostly Spanish.

"Ortiz," I told her.

"Where are your people from?"

"San Luis."

"Valley people, uh. You work?"

"I work," I said.

"Are you Catholic?" She laughed.

I looked for Angie. I noticed that the woman's hair was thin, exposing dark flesh beneath dirty silver strands.

"Ahh," she exclaimed, throwing up her hands. "Goddamn kids today! Goddamn kids don't know their own language!"

Angie translated before we sat down for dinner at the card table and apologized. As I ate, the old woman exchanged her cigar for a small pipe, and the room filled with a pungent, cherry tobacco smell.

"Disgraciado," the old woman said.

"Not this one, *Abuelita*. He saved me," Angie said, serving me a plate. "I would have had to walk."

"Women should be with the fathers of their babies." The *Abuelita* argued with no one in particular over large plates of fried potatoes and red *chile*. "People had religion," the old woman continued. "But today," she said, shaking her head, "they have no God."

"My *Abuelito* used to be religious," Angie apologized. "She thinks we all have to be crazy for Jesus."

"It's in you," the *Abuelita* interrupted. She was still huffing on the pipe.

"What does she mean? In you?" I asked.

"My *Abuelito* used to be *Penitente*."

"What?" My mouth was filled with tortilla. I hadn't eaten anything home-cooked in over six months.

"Eh?" the old woman jumped, a slight spasm.

"He asked you what is *Pentitente, Abuelita*?" Angie said, louder.

"Good men," the *Abuelita* said. "That's what they were."

I gave Angie a perplexed look. I didn't stop eating, though.

"You like the food, eh?" The old woman pointed at my plate.

"Very good," I said, taking another large mouthful of mashed beans and red chile.

"They were an order of men in New Mexico. Men who worked in the mines there," she explained. "They'd get together during *Lenten*."

"During what?"

"They got together during Easter-time and would perform ceremonies," Angie explained.

"What kind of ceremonies?" I asked.

"Penance," the old woman said. She hadn't touched a thing on her plate. She just sat and attended to her pipe.

"Nobody really knows," Angie continued. "They would stay out on the *llano* for weeks. Read scripture and give each other penance."

"Penance," the old woman repeated.

"They say that they would make each other suffer, you know, for their sins or faith or whatever." Angie shrugged. "I guess you gotta believe in that shit. Be Catholic," she said, smiling at me.

"Jesus," I said.

"Yes," the old woman added in English.

"Crazy," Angie observed, making slow circles around her ear with a fork. "That's where the crucifix came from. In the living room. They had 'em up in the *moradas*."

"Good men," the old woman repeated.

"Crazy," Angie said. "That's why I'm not Catholic anymore."

"They never left me when I was pregnant," the old woman said.

Angie didn't say another word and was quiet until I helped her with the dishes. She apologized again for her *Abuelita*. "She just wants me to leave," Angie told me. "She wants me follow after Benito no matter what. Chase him around. You know how it is." She explained how Benito had become close to the old woman. Angie explained how the old woman liked Benito at first because he threw out the garbage, fixed up her Tempo. The *Abuelita* even went so far as to say it was good to have a man around the house.

"What's keeping you from leaving?" I asked her.

"He's a fuck." After further probing and a few more cigarettes, I learned that the fuck had been in and out of the Youth Offender System in Colorado City since the age of sixteen. That road began with a few minor offenses ranging from siphoning gasoline, to selling his mother's jewelry. Later he stole some parts for a few customizations, which is where Luis probably met him. Benito had passed from that life, though, after he met Angie. Things were working until one day in January when his brother Lloyd bought a truck, and Benito decided to make the move. Angie tried to stop him, but Benito was drinking beer and took a baseball bat to her. Benito didn't leave a letter or a phone message. He decided it would be best just to leave after the beating. "It didn't hurt that much, but no fuck of a man is going to do that to me, father or no father," Angie declared, shaking her head. "He never really had a problem leaving the baby, you know."

The walls leading down to her bedroom were wood paneled, and the stacked mattresses that made up her bed rested on a concrete floor. One simple dresser in the windowless, dank room.

Angie sat on the bed and lit a cigarette. "Talk to me, I'm bored," she said. "Tell me something."

"What?"

"I don't know. Something. Tell me about the Army."

"How can you live down here?" I asked, staring up at the single exposed bulb that was the basement's only light.

"You can get used to all kinds of things," Angie said. "You travel much, like in the commercials?"

"I've been overseas a couple of times."

"I haven't been out of Colorado," Angie said. "Well, my mother went to Hawaii once to meet my father at a naval base but that was about it. I was like, five or six, I think. Very little and don't remember nothing. I think I was in Alabama once too. I've seen pictures. Where were you?"

"Macedonia," I said. "In the mud."

"Sick."

"You get used to it. You learn to stomach all kinds of awful things."

"What things?"

"Little things. Like sleeping in a squat. You get more sleep if you sit up in your poncho up against your pack or a tree. Got to get used to it. Only thing you can do."

"Sounds pretty sick."

"You can get used to all kinds of things," I said, smiling, following the cracks in the unfinished ceiling. "You see your father ever?" I said.

She looked straight at me. "What the hell do I want to see him for?"

"Sorry," I said.

"What about you?" Angie asked.

"I got a daughter in California."

"Why aren't you out there?"

"I don't know," I said. "I got stationed here in Fort Carson and just never went back."

"What's her name?"

It had been a while since I had mouthed the words. "Belle."

Suddenly Angie was leaning towards me, touching me with her perfect hands and kissing the side of my face. Then our lips touched, and my stomach moved. She swept over my neck and shoulder to pull off my tie and shirt. The dress she was wearing came off over her head. I quickly learned her contours, her legs and thighs. I followed birthmarks and pock scars with my bitten fingernails. I followed them, mutely tasting the memory of my wife. The marks turned into flower tattoos down to the small of her back, and in my head I connected them, filling in the blanks down to her waist and thighs. She lifted a bit to help me maneuver under her. Our bellies were somewhat mismatched, groin to groin. I wondered out loud if this was safe, and she giggled. "Jesus, Relles," she said. "I'm pregnant, not dead."

That first night, Angie prayed with the glow-in-the-dark Rosary beads hanging on her bed post. I thought she was asleep, yet she pulled herself out of bed, in the small, sleepless hours around two or three in the morning. Naked, she kneeled, her hands clasped tightly, and I thought I heard her whispering. It was too dark for me to tell for sure. I pretended to be asleep.

Over crumpled sheets, Angie was sitting Indian-style on the bed, busy tracing the small tattoos on my forearms and the Navajo tribal patterns that made up the purple sleeves. "I feel comfortable with you," she said in an amorous murmur, biting her lower lip. "Can I show you something?"

"Sure."

"You won't freak?" she asked, hunching forward, elbows between her legs.

"That depends, I guess," I said. "On what you show me, I mean."

She pulled the comforter from her bed and pulled the yellow sunflower print around her large belly and thin frame, exposing her small breasts for a long minute. I waited while she moved to the dresser catty-corner from the bed. The antiqued top was full of knick-knacks and picture frames with unfamiliar faces. A large wooden box sat covered with a lace doily, neatly to one edge of the dresser. She moved a black and white picture to get to the large case.

She dropped the box on my lap, the weight heavy and awkward, taking me by surprise. I sat confused as I flipped the metal binding that held it shut to find the shiny contents. In the box rested a large-barreled weapon, a nickel-plated .50 caliber revolver. The inside of the case was a plush red and looked specially made for the piece and the fifteen rounds points-up in the box.

"It was my father's," she said. "He used to be a Sheriff's Deputy in Huérfano County. *Abuelita* didn't want me to have it. She hates these things, but my mom gave it to me after the fuck came at me."

"You ever fire it?" I asked.

"Hell yeah. Gotta get the brain anchored down but I can fire it." She smiled, pushing aside the wild, red mass that was her hair.

"It'll break your wrist."

"The fuck and his brothers won't mess with me again, you know. As long as I have this."

"You're hard, no?" I said giving the piece back to her.

"Yeah," she answered.

With the gun between us I held her, and we lay there reliant on one another's bodies.

I was wide awake when the fuck arrived. It was Sunday morning and I'd made some coffee. Angie was still asleep.

"Open the door, Angelita!" the fuck screamed. "Jesus, Jesus, Jesus!" he repeated.

"Goddamm boys are no good for anything," the *Abuelita* said, frozen. It was almost a whisper.

Benito was young and red-eyed. I thought the acne-scarred face belonged to Luis or my brother. He was not wearing a shirt, just a simple pair of faded jeans, broad shoulders, large and round.

"And what kind of fuck are you?" he yelled through the dirty glass. Maybe he didn't know me by name, but he knew what was happening in this old house, and in that small basement.

"I'm a friend of Angie's," I replied.

"You're a thief!" he snarled. "Come on, thief! Open the Goddamn door!"

I pulled the chain from the door and put my bare feet out onto the porch. The blood ran faster through my head.

The *Abuelita* and Angie were behind me as I rushed out onto the porch. I don't remember why I went out there. I saw four glaring characters, Benito and his crew. Each one looked as young and tired as the next. They punched at me. Benito dragged me farther by the arm into the open space of the concrete porch. He crushed at my head and chest. My knees buckled. They clawed at me, kicking at me in fragmented movements at my back. They pushed my face down into the concrete. There was nothing stopping them from killing me.

I couldn't see the whole goodbye because the blood and snot had smeared on my face and started to harden in the late morning sun. I sat on the ground like a fool, and didn't dare move. I thought I might break. I do remember Benito leaning on the horn for Angie to come as she hugged her *Abuelita*.

Later, the old woman helped me lean into the stucco wall to catch my balance, holding my arm until I could stand. "It's funny," the *Penitente's* wife said, "how God wants you,"—and the rest stands as something that has taken me years to translate—, "and then He don't."

11. JUANITA'S BOY

"If I'm going to be staying here, *Hijos*," Mitedio said, watching the crew of boys, their shabby clothes, bare feet and stained t-shirts, "then we need to get the ground rules straight, no?" The boys marched through the living room to their beloved Uncle and laughed at his wide, bald scalp, how he flattened across the last remaining hairs. "And, *sabes que, Mihijos*," he said, "the rules are we must attend the dog track in the morning and earn enough money to attend the Mexican movies. Those are the rules."

The boys, Relles and Neto and even the crew of fosters, yelled and agreed. He told them their *Jefe* and *Jefita* had abandoned them for the week. He did not explain that their *Abuelita* in New Mexico turned up dead-meat and buried. Instead he pulled a bottle from his coverall pocket and took a long, passionate kiss. He called for the youngest Ortiz boy.

"What, *Tio*?"

"Are you getting smaller and smaller?"

"I'm growing, *Tio*," little Neto said, and the boy held his arms up to show the tiny mounds that would one day be biceps.

The next morning the boys ate a breakfast of fried bologna and fried potatoes before climbing into the bed of the Ranchero. They headed for dollar bills owed from Joey Aguilar's house. He wasn't home, but a fat, ancient hand served the cash through a window.

Next, the crew drove out to the fairgrounds and the swap meet, and Mitedio had a conversation with a woman, her long, black hair parted down the center and eyebrows drawn in an arc. She stared and shook her head, threw her hand onto a corduroy hip. "Jesus. What you doing, Mitedio? You stealing kids now?"

"My brother's kids."

She asked, "Your mama?"

"Dead."

"What happened? I'm sorry, Mitedio."

"She's just dead."

"You see, *Mihijos*," Mitedio explained from behind the wheel, "at a casino you bet against the house. And, when you bet against the house, the odds are pretty bad. You know that? Any man has to know that."

"Yes, *Tio*."

"It's all French. You know French? 'Pari-mutuel', *Hijo*s," Mitedio explained. "It's French. It's a wager and not a bet. What do they teach you in that school?"

The boys said nothing. Their mouths were open wide until the oldest, Relles, finally asked, "What does that mean?"

"Mean?" Mitedio said. "Well, it means you win better. It means you are not playing the house, but you are playing the betters. *Los* Agents. That's what it means."

"*Es eso* Agents?"

"Agents. You know agents. Here you make your own luck. Here a man can know his numbers and know his runners and win. And we're men who win, no?"

"The *Jefe* says you can't win gambling. He says you should focus on a paycheck and earn your way."

"Oh, *Mihijo*!" Mitedio said, grinning. "Your father has mouths to feed and cannot bet. But we have no children. Neto, do we have children?"

Neto shook his head, dumbly.

"We have no children, Relles. And that means we can take our risks," Mitedio answered. "We can go to the daily double with our ten dollars and triple our money if we know the runners. I don't have a house to take care of. I am independent and free from all of those, *Mihijo*. Once a man has a paycheck and a job he loses all his freedoms."

"But a man needs to work, right? *Tio*?" Relles insisted. "It's not right to do this in the middle of the week."

"Oh, *Hijo*," Mitedio answered.

The daily double started promptly at noon, and Mitedio and the crew were the first in line. Children must be supervised at all times, was what the ticket agent told Mitedio as he talked and talked. He purchased candy bars and sat to study his Race Program.

Mitedio explained: "Gotta find a runner, *Mihijos*. Gotta find the right one for us."

And it took him nearly five minutes of study, but he found a runner called "Juanita's Boy." He decided to pass on another called "Short Nothing."

"He's won at this time slot every day last week," Mitedio said. "This is the time for him. This is the time." He grinned and ran to the betting agent with the boys. He waited and staggered across the betting lines, and he threw down all of his dollar bills, saving absolutely nothing for the day or for any amount of "in-cases" or "what-ifs".

"The start don't matter none," Mitedio instructed, gathering the boys around. "It's the stretch, *Hijos*, that matters. The stretch call is what matters. That's when we'll see if 'Juanita's Boy' is the closer we're looking for. The last stretch."

"I don't think you picked the right dog, *Tio*."

"Shut it, Relles. You're just like your old man. You gotta trust the handicap. You gotta trust it. It's about following the numbers, boy. It's about watching the dogs and the races closely. Whether the dog is a closer or a breaker. It's about watching positions and the first three dogs that cross. That's all it is. Goddamn it. I'm wasting my words."

The boys got the *Tio*'s buzz. They began whooping and hollering. They screamed out the dog's name.

"What's the stretch, *Tio*?"

"Shut it, Neto," Mitedio said. "Shut the hell up when a man is concentrating and thinking. Go, son! Go! Now's the time, son! Go, son!"

In a couple of minutes, as he drained his beers and spit at his own feet, Mitedio does not confess to the crew of boys he chose "Juanita's Boy" because the mother's middle name was Juanita, and so he had to put the money down on this day of her funeral. That was his duty as a son.

"What happened, Mitedio? What happened?" the boys said in another minute after the booming voice announced a "no-race."

"It seems," Mitedio said, "the dog has done up and died, *Hijos*. Ran into the *pinche* rabbit and then the fence and had to be put down. That's what it looks like. Sometimes it happens. The races are not for soft dogs."

One of the fosters began crying over the dog, crying for lost Juanita's Boy.

"Don't cry, *Hijos*," Mitedio pleaded. "No-race means our dollar bills will be returned to us. It means we'll get our money and we'll go to the Mexican Movies. First, though, we'll put more money down. A man always puts more money down so quit your damn crying. You want the money out there, don't you? For the movies?"

"But what about our dog, *Tio?*"

After the third race the crew miraculously had money for the Mexican movies over on 4th street. Mitedio weighed his bets more carefully, saving dollar bills for admission, hot dogs and RC Colas.

Mitedio liked the Riverside Drive-In or the Mesa Drive-In, but mostly he liked "the 96" downtown because they allowed little *mocos* in the truck bed.

Mitedio directed Relles to place the speaker on the driver side window and control the volume, and the crew was jealous.

"Why does he get the front?" Neto and the fosters asked.

"Because I say," Mitedio answered, "and because he is the oldest. Now, pay attention, boys. They show your people's movies. You have to learn your language. *Español? Tu sabes?* It's a damn shame in the garage you boys speak such shitty Spanish. Your Great Grandfather would be rolling in his grave to know his people couldn't follow what he said."

And that was how Mitedio saw the Mexican movies, as school for the boys.

"These movies are about life, *Hijos*," Mitedio lectured. "You watch them close and you'll learn a lesson about your lives."

Mostly they liked the classics, *puro classicos*, the westerns of Pedro Infante with his singing, partying and his womanizing, his *charro* crooning. The crew couldn't follow the plot, but they liked the action of *Los Hijos de Maria Morales*. Mitedio liked the cornball jokes.

"You know I met him in California," Mitedio said before he downed his hot dog and drained his rum and RC Cola.

Relles asked, "Who, *Tio?*"

"Pedro Infantes."

"You never met him."

"I swear I met him," Mitedio claimed. "In California. I swear. I was with my *Tio* working in the fields and he came to talk to the workers. We all saw him." Mitedio was in love with those songs and those movies, reminding him of growing up in New Mexico. Reminding him of his people and of his dead family.

The concessions saved the crew of boys, Relles and Neto. The foot longs and the hamburgers. Arms full of RC Cola bottles and hot buttered popcorn. Soft pretzels, sno-cones and pizza slices. Endless strings of rope licorice alongside boxed candies.

"Rich, flavorful and satisfying," little Neto repeated from the intermission trailers.

After the first feature, just before the end of the second, Mitedio took off his boots and put his stinking feet up on the dash. His body ached like a cavity so he banished Relles to the back of the Ranchero with his brothers. And, finally, when the crew, wrapped up in Mitedio's old horse blankets, had pulled off their sneaks and snuggled up next to the tire wells, Mitedio could finally think without bother or question. This was the time Pedro Infante crackled through the speaker and wailed *Las Mananitas*, and the time *Tio* sobbed for Juanita's Boy. He held the speaker, turned up the volume to maximum, until the warm voices were all the boys heard.

12. *DESCANSOS*

The first man I'd met while working maintenance became my friend and gave me a place to sleep in his basement out on La Vega Road. He shared *posole* and mashed beans with me at his dinner table and he drove me around town looking for fluorescent liquor signs out on Central, Northern and East Ninth.

This one evening, this one time, while we were drinking beer, I asked him, "How much longer you gonna fuck around with that car?"

"A man works to keep himself," he instructed.

The half-primer, half-purple Chevy was a '76 and the first beautiful thing I'd seen after the Army. At first I didn't want it, at first I didn't want the responsibility. His wife and kid landed up dead-meat in the thing out on Interstate 25 near Aguilar, Colorado about two years back.

After we drank as much as we could, we drove out to the crash site and just pulled over, turned off the engine. Luis' eyes flooded and he doubled over with yearning. He was bulky and shaped like an ox and it was strange to see him cry. Headlights streamed by and I stared at the sad wooden cross and roses to the side of the highway, the wallet-sized photos and an old locket placed beneath.

He ended it by making the sign of the cross and saying, "*Descansos por los muertos.*"

That Monte Carlo was a piece of shit afterwards, mangled and smashed. But his work had an amazing effect. He dropped a new Windsor V8 and banged out all the dents to smooth the body. He lowered the suspension and fixed her up with a new set of basket rims, all chrome and clean.

"It's drivable," Luis answered. "You can drive it."

"Well, that's the point, right?"

His shoulders slumped. "It's not about selling a damn car." He wiped his long forehead with his ancient fingers, shifted his cigarette from underneath his moustache.

While I packed up my stuff, Luis airbrushed the figure of a woman. He introduced the hood of that Chevy as a vision. I didn't know Luis as an artist. I'd never been around one. I saw the woman had angel wings, but her eyes seemed gray and cold, her flawless arms crossed low at her waist.

I took Luis' car and went looking for Romes and found him sitting in a squatter's house with his hair combed back and his collar up, suffering through the cold of a New Mexico night. He looked strung out and thin. I really thought he was in jail or dead.

I put my hand on Romes' thin shoulder and took the cigarette out of his mouth. "How'd you ever imagine finding me, Manito?" he asked.

He was the only one laughing. Out of everyone at the party, he was the only one laughing.

"I'm heading out to California," I told him.

"A lifetime ago, Manito. I was in Colorado a lifetime ago." He smiled widely with big, yellow teeth.

People were always fixing him drinks, rolling the fattest blunts to get him to slow down, making him talk while they quickly guzzled. The people at this particular party, this particular night, I didn't know very well, and I was confident they didn't know Romes all that well either. He told me he had just lost his house and his common law wife.

I told him, "I know the kid's out there somewhere, you know."

He shook his head furiously as if he had been there with me the whole way, every mile. "What kid is that, Manito?"

"My kid."

We started telling stories about Army days. We talked about Camp Bondsteel and the 7th Infantry. At one time my brother had tried to explain it all to me, but this night I was out of luck. I came all that way and the bastard kept it hidden.

"The Army is over for me and you," he finally told me. "I know that much."

Only the drinking and the weed came out that night. He was in high spirits after receiving his latest VA check and he showed me his wallet and the ten twenty dollar bills he had left. At this moment, while on that disgusting little couch, as he rested the money out on his lap, I noticed how his curly hair was clean, how things were going to be all right for him for the next couple of days, until the money ran out.

"Shit happened a long time ago, Manito. Two years ago, whatever. So don't ask me no more, Manito. Jesus. Jesus. Jesus! Don't ask me," he repeated and then he laughed at himself.

Romes kept talking and sounded glorious: he told a fifteen-year-old girl that he was working in Taos as a vendor at a baseball field, and then he told another woman whose face I never saw he was living closer to the mountains and restoring old cars. He asked another girl if he could sleep at her apartment, and then he told another junky-looking girl who was fighting with her boyfriend to meet him in the narrow street out front and to forget about the little *chivato* she had come with, that he had a custom Monte Carlo outside.

"Just let me borrow the car, *Cabrón*."

After a day and a half, California came like speed trials. I drove Luis' death-filled Chevy all night and stopped only to eat, then once to piss at the head of an entrance ramp. I was high on amphetamines my brother Romes gave me in New Mexico and I wasn't used to driving.

I stopped in an AM/PM for gas, gave my troubles a case of Bud Light. The woman's face behind the counter was veiled in bulletproof glass. The tattoo of an eastern sun on her neck lit the wall. Her nametag read "Lynn." "If we were in love," I asked, "would you ever leave me?"

The Chevy fell into park, and the brakes cried in front of Loretta's house that morning, our house on Cardinal Avenue. All the houses on the block were flat roofed and earth-toned and built by the same company, but this house stood out because it sat inside an immense garden. She loved the beauty and the neighbors would always admire her roses and marigolds. Once I took a shortcut through the garden in a straight line for the door, and Loretta said, "Can't you see that's disrespectful?"

I managed the steps to our home's front door. It was missing a screen, so I reached my hand through to feel the knob. The metal felt cold and reminded me of loneliness, so I rang the bell three or four times. I looked in through the living room window; there were no curtains and I saw toys on the floor: a little plastic kitchen and a spotted horse on springs.

I smashed a window.

Inside, the green carpeting in the hall to the bedrooms was stained, and I could feel the blood pumping through me. Loretta's bedroom was cluttered and sad. The door frame had been fixed from when she locked herself in, and a queen-sized waterbed now filled the room. Two antique-looking dressers stood side by side near the closet. Work clothes were stacked neatly on her bed. A necklace rested on one of the dressers. I held the metal in my hands smelling for perfume.

I sniffed around like a dog, continuing through her jewelry. I found some photos, the faces in them all strange until the Polaroids taken just before I left for Macedonia, and a copy of one of the pictures of my daughter Belle that I had kept in my wallet.

I pocketed some money from a jewelry box, about fifty dollars folded into a small square. It took me a while to notice the man's work shirts hanging on the door to the closet, but the gray material looked pressed, with the top button done up with care. The logo over the pocket read Allied Electric.

In the photo, my daughter Belle posed in front of a large tree. Her clothes were too big for her frame, and her face was mischievously young and rosy, her perfect nose like her mother's. In another, newer photo, a young man stood in front of the house, a handsome man with a white face and a red beard, smiling wide, patiently waiting for the picture to be taken.

Around the corner from our bedroom, I edged to where our daughter slept. Toys lined the dirty carpet of the small room, and I had to clear a little path to get into the center. Her books littered the long shelf over the picture window, looking out into the back yard.

The walls up to about four feet were an institutional brown. The color reminded me of the room at the halfway house, but here brown meant a prairie and rolling hills, the sky meeting them at the level of the bookshelf and the dresser that held my daughter's clothes.

The blue horizon blended into majestic purples and turquoises, fields rolling backwards into hills and then finally mountains, and then on to amazing distances, billowing, cloud-filled horizons over the twin bed. I lost myself in view of those faultless clouds, along the tops of trees that extended on the walls and some white picket fences added for detail over the brown hills. Then I rested on my daughter's bed and the light fixture poured warm sunshine over me.

The mailman placed the mail. The phone rang a couple of times. I felt sick and weak and had to vomit in their bathroom. And in that lowliness I became the worst thoughts.

I held the .32 Romes had given me in case of trouble. I had the gun in my front pocket, and every once in a while I would pull it out. There were no bullets so I kept pulling back the hammer and letting myself have it. My eyes squeezed shut and warm tears cut down my face.

If I regret anything from that day it's that Loretta's hair wasn't down. "Jesus. I can smell the fuckin' beer on you." She shook her head with terror.

She eyed the gun and before I could say a word she had the phone. "Can you even imagine in your stupid fuckin' head what I have to do to explain to your daughter where you have been and what the hell you have been doin'?" Her round face had no makeup whatsoever, pure as a saint. Her skin remained close to porcelain.

"Loretta, I've moved on."

"You hear me, Goddamn it? Goddamn it! You see?" she said. "You fuck of a man."

I dragged her to me and my muscles began to spasm. That's when I could feel what was alive in her, that pregnant belly. I squeezed her arm down to the bone. With those blue skies around me, I swear I wanted to hurt her. I wanted to break both her Goddamned arms.

She jerked from me into the hallway. The threads tore down her shirt. I grabbed at her shoulder and then at her hair.

"Ah, please Retta," I repeated, still holding the gun. "Shit. Fuck. God."

When I saw my wife pulling away from me and running out the door in a full, short-legged sprint, still bawling, I knew our goodbyes would never be real, that they would have to stay inside.

After two or three days of me haunting around Retta's neighborhood, they hauled me out in front of a Denny's. As the officers had the cuffs on me, between parked cars, and as they draped my body over the trooper's hood, for several less-than-conscious moments, I pleaded with the woman on Luis' Monte Carlo and her naked, airbrushed frame.

13. A ROCK IN THE BEANS

A rock in the beans split the *Tio* Mitedio's tooth right in half down to the nerve. The boys watched the man wail and holler right at the dinner table: "Look what your wife did to me and to my soul. God-damn women are trying to kill me."

And their *Jefe* was quick to laugh: "Your soul?"

The *Jefe* and his boys, littlest Neto, Relles and the crew of fosters, saw Mitedio punch at the *Jefita*. The man grabbed at her hair and apron, holding her with cement hands. "*Puta*. Whore." They saw their *Jefita*, their only caretaker, landing on her tail bone as their *Jefe* defended the woman and ripped the *Tio*'s clothes and skin. They viewed it all through the lowlight of early evening as the sun drained from the kitchen, and the boys waited to see who would be the first to flip on the bare bulb above the table.

To the boys it was as if two great giants were tussling, like in the myths they read in old Miss Martinez's Bessemer School classroom, two great forces colliding and falling through the back screen door and onto cement patio, over the wrought iron picnic table and the laundry basin. The voices and blows echoed out to the alley and rose to the street lamps.

"This is why Mama didn't ever want you around no more," the *Jefe* yelled. He kicked at the man as they went toe to toe. "Because of shit like this."

"Fuck you, Bro," Mitedio cried. "And your Goddamn *pinche* beans. Your shitty little house."

"You're lucky to have those Goddamn beans," the *Jefe* wailed as he slapped Mitedio's face and head. "You're lucky to have my woman feed you. Any woman feeding you."

And the boys swore they saw the *Jefe* holding a pistol, a dark-barreled piece of metal pointing towards the *Tio* and later at the *Tio*'s Ranchero. They swore they heard the lightning and the crash. The *Jefe* pronounced, "In all your life stay off my Goddamn property."

Mitedio's story was that he drove out to the east side apartment of a woman he knew. Maybe Melda Q or Bernarda L: *cabrónas* who lived at the bars.

For days and days Mitedio slept on strange couches and pull-outs as he nursed that tooth, his only treatment his bottle and his special herb to smoke. He kept it hidden from the neighborhood, and months later, after the madness of those outcast days, Mitedio blamed those beans. As if a meal made it all go wrong for the man in Colorado. As if that tooth was the only pain that drove Mitedio to steal dollar bills.

And the police called looking for Mitedio, asking if he'd been around. Sometimes the phone rang and it was Mitedio himself, so the *Jefe* slammed the phone down after challenging him to come and see what waited for him. And sometimes Melda Q or whoever was the *puta* of the month called on behalf of Mitedio and spoke to the *Jefita*. Usually she asked for forgiveness and money, mostly money. And the *Jefe* would speak for a while and tell the woman to get right with God and then hang up, after ripping the phone from his wife's hand. "Goddamn it, *Mujer*. I don't want that man or his women calling here. Brother or no brother."

Sometimes Mitedio called and got the boys, found them at home without the *Jefe*. Promised them fishing and road trips to San Luis, an endless amount of hunting excursions. Miles and miles of open *llano* for the man and his favorite boys.

"We got food for you, *Tio*," the boys called into the receiver. "We got money and we know where the *Jefe* has his cigarettes, *Tio*. The house is all empty for you, *Tio*. It's all waiting."

The rivalry between Neto and Relles began much earlier in their lives than that summer the *Tio* Mitedio disappeared. The boys were more at odds, more at each other's throats than normal that season and even that entire year. That was the year of the stabbing. The year little Neto grabbed a toothpick and jabbed it into his brother's wrist. The blood spilled over the rivalry that began in backyards and around the barking dogs of the neighborhood as the boys screamed and yelled for each other's pain.

The fights became so frequent even the *Jefe* and the *Jefita* mentioned it, in the middle of the night when the radio and the TV shut down and the work of sleep and resting were the only chores of the house.

"The boys only get into it when they have no work to do," the *Jefe* said. "There's just nothing to do about it. That's what boys do."

"Oh, that's just what boys do, huh?"

"Yes. Exactly like I say. That is what they do."

"Boys don't stab one another."

"Me and Mitedio would throw *chingazos* in the house and the *Abuelita* would come at us with the broom and clear us out," the *Jefe* argued. "Chase us out into the fields and that was how it was."

"*Su familia* was like animals. Like monsters."

"It's in the blood, *Cabróna*."

"Well, it is *your* blood. *Your* people and not mine. So long as you know it ain't my blood."

"Ah, *Mujer*," the *Jefe* said.

"I can only forgive so much, so help me God."

"What the hell do you know anyway? Come on over here."

"I tell you it will be the end of my boys. You are laughing but soon you will be crying. Mark my words, *Viejo*."

"You to blame, Neto," Relles said the morning when the Jefe had them up on the ladder and up on the roof to tar the leaks and to clean the gutters. "You the one who got the *Tio* kicked out."

"Shut up. You always saying that."

"I saw you bring the beans to the *Jefita* and I saw you helping her. I know you soaked them. It was your chore and you the one to blame."

"I hate you, Relles."

"I seen you run from them *Cocos* in the basement when you get the beans. When you get the potatoes for the Jefita. I seen you with my own eyes running from the basement."

"Shut up! I was just doing what I was told, Relles. I didn't mean to do nothing to the *Tio* and to start nothing."

"You probably put the rock in the beans. Didn't you, Neto?"

"Quit saying that."

And that was the day they all referred to as simply "the fall." The day Relles cracked his head backwards off of the ladder. The day Neto was blamed for cracking the brother's head, for not caring for his brother. The day Neto was given the burden of credit for hurting and harming the brother. A hundred miles of pain little Neto walked for years and years to come.

Neto remembered the river of blood and mucus on the concrete, the headache of watching his brother being dragged and held by the *Jefe*. The view of the man running and the ride to St. Mary Corwin. Blood from the head onto the interior of the old truckito and the *Jefe's* white t-shirt.

He heard the words: "Be still. Be still, boy." Neto remembered sitting in the waiting room with the TV chained to the floor and watching the local newscasts alongside his *Jefe*. That was the day little Neto was made responsible for his brother's entire life. And years later when the news came to the house that Relles died after a crash site, his Monte

Carlo smashed and mangled at the corner of 8th and Abriendo, Neto remembered that feeling of his brother's life slipping from him like arms and legs from a ladder.

Neto and the crew of fosters were looking at the nudie book Mitedio had given Neto for his birthday when they heard the lock click on the front door. Instantly, Neto shoved the book in between the bed and the concrete foundation, and the fosters ran back to their bed and Neto slammed down rigidly. They listened to the *Jefe*'s footsteps and followed him moving from room to room, the bathroom and kitchen.

"You get us in to trouble every day, Neto," the fosters said.

"Mitedio reads these all the time. That's what men do. He told me."

The *Jefe* came down the stairs, his eyes red from drinking and the smell of *cigarillos* on his flannel shirt. The boys all watched him come in and sit down by the dresser.

"What are you boys doing down here?" the *Jefe* asked.

No one said a word. Then Neto twitched nervously and sat up in a pretty guilty move. The *Jefe* blew his nose and then returned the handkerchief to his coverall pocket. His hands were greasy from his *truckito*'s brake job.

"You miss your *Tio*, huh?" the *Jefe* asked, and took the boys by surprise.

The boys kept still and didn't dare answer. The *Jefe* lit a cigarette and blew smoke rings into the unfinished ceiling of floor board and ply wood.

"I know how much you love him," the *Jefe* said. "I see the way he is with you."

The boys looked at their *Jefe* patiently; they seemed certain of bad news. The *Jefe* coming down to talk meant either work coming or bad news, and with the day in the *campos* over and done there could only be bad news coming.

What the boys didn't know was *Tio* Mitedio had been caught with some property. How much would never be known to the boys, but what they did know was that the *Jefe* had been contacted about sentencing and about *Tio* Mitedio turning himself in. The *Jefe* could never tell the boys or his wife the details, but he felt he owed the boys words. His third beer gave him the will to let them in on the horrible news.

"Just the same," the *Jefe* said. "He's going away for a while and won't be watching you any time soon."

"Why?" Neto asked and the fosters followed.

"And I thought you should know," the *Jefe* answered.

Lying back on the cot Neto almost turned away. Put his arm over his eyes while the fosters sat up to listen. "What have they done to him?" Neto managed to ask. There were tear streaks down Neto's cheeks as he spoke.

"They put him in jail," the *Jefe* answered.

Neto's eyes opened. He stared at the ceiling. "You turned him out and now he's going away forever," he said.

"Your *Tio* steals and can't stay straight, Neto."

"Mitedio is a war hero and has been around the world," the boy answered.

"Mitedio is a thief and has a habit, boy. Now he is going away and I wanted you to know."

"And now you want us to hate him!" Neto yelled. "And I'll never hate him!"

"Neto."

"I'll never hate him!"

For the drive out to Colorado State Penitentiary, the entire family crammed into the bench seat of the *truckito*. Normally, the boys jumped into the *truckito*'s bed and had to fend for themselves. The drive was thirty, maybe even forty miles, skies were gray and after a night filled with rain, stayed overcast. The *Jefita* argued for her boys to stay close and dry.

"It's not even raining no more," the *Jefe* said. And then finally, "If that is what you want, *Mujer*. It will be tight."

Neto pressed his nose up against the cold glass. It was always better to be heading away from the fields of work in Vineland, he thought. The day held more possibility.

"Don't mark up all the damn windows, Neto," the *Jefe* warned. The *Jefe* found on long trips like this he couldn't focus, that he was too distracted by fighting and yelling. The decibels rose as the scenery of prairie and dark brown and green-tinted hills beyond the closed window became more interesting and exciting for the boys.

He couldn't stand the incessant fighting and questions:

"Where are we going, *Jefe*? Can we stop soon? How far are we driving? What is this town called, *Jefe*?"

"You'll know soon enough, Goddamn it," the *Jefe* answered.

"Be patient, boys," the *Jefita* said.

It was the flat, empty country passing by like a great turntable, that the strangeness of the trip crept into little Neto. And even though he sat in his *Jefita*'s lap, and she held him close around the waist, he still sat nervous and leaned back against his *Jefita*'s breast. He thought about seeing his *Tio* and what he might say or how he would look at the beloved man in Canon City blues. He daydreamed about the long, lazy afternoons out fishing or out driving with Mitedio, and he grew more and more nervous until his fingers slid down his arms and into his palms.

The *Jefe*'s foot grew heavier, the *truckito* growled ahead, and more of the rolling hills were revealed. Neto's stomach turned and rolled. His face began to whiten and he turned to look at his *Jefita* to reveal his queasiness.

"Goddamn it, Neto," the *Jefe* barked. "I could let you out here so we can pick you up on the way back."

"Don't listen to him, Neto," the *Jefita* whispered in her faintest voice. She rubbed the boy's belly under his button up shirt and white t-shirt. "You're coming along with us no matter what."

His stomach felt rougher around the Fremont overpass. The *Jefe* had to stop the *truckito* so Neto could climb over the fosters and his brother Relles to vomit on the side of the road. Relles laughed as the boy tipped his head and made heaving noises.

"Jesus Christ," the *Jefe* snarled.

The boy came staggering and stumbling over the weeds and foliage to the side of the road. He vomited again, and then a third time, just missing his own shoes and his own pant leg. Out the open door, the *Jefe*'s voice: "Goddamn it, Neto. Don't fucking puke on yourself. *Cabrón!*"

"Can't seem to keep nothing in his stomach," the *Jefita* said, climbing out the door. She eased to Neto's side and then down on one knee despite being in a summer dress or the sharp gravel stabbing at her skin. She pushed at the boy's high collar to save it. She had her handkerchief to the boy's lips and face, she rubbed his stomach. The passenger side door swung wide open and the crew of fosters and Relles hung out into the afternoon air.

"Are we gonna stay here all damn day or what?" the *Jefe* said in disgust.

The *Jefita* stayed at her son's side, wiping at his forehead. And because of the hour of the morning her own stomach began to churn and her throat began to heave and convulse. She had wondered when the morning stomach aches might come, the suffering of a raw stomach and digestion.

"How are you doing?" the *Jefita* asked after she vomited by her son's side. "How's your *pansa*, Neto?" The *Jefita* worked as best she could with her handkerchief, moistened the tip with rainwater building in the cracks of the gravel highway before scrubbing one last time at her son's face.

At one point the boy and the *Jefita* turned from the roadway; the pungent sprinkle of rain felt fresher and cleaner. All around were signs telling just how far they were from home.

"It's so beautiful out here in the rain," the *Jefita* told the boy.

The *Jefe* raised his head from the rolled-down window and motioned to his wristwatch: "We gotta move, Goddamn it. We're burning the morning."

The *Jefita* looked at the *Jefe*, gathering up her purse.

"Don't pay no attention to your *Jefe*," the woman repeated, combing and parting the boy's hair with her fingers. "He ain't going nowhere without his Neto or without me."

The boy grinned and leaned into her.

"I remember once when my *Jefe* was driving me out to the festivals in Alamosa," the *Jefita* said. "I remember getting so sick and throwing up all my breakfast, and the old man, the Grandfather of yours I mean, was so mad at me. You hear me, Neto?"

The boy nodded.

"And that man growled at me like a damn fool, and you know what I did, Neto?"

The boy shook his head.

"I just stood and got myself together and gave him as good I as I got. You know what I mean, *Mihijo*."

Mitedio's inmate number was 34631 and the *Jefe* repeated it before he slapped at his chest for the pen and notebook he carried. He had to write that number down in his black book to remember. He replaced it over his heart and behind the cigarettes he carried which made him feel like smoking though it wasn't permitted in the penitentiary offices.

The *Jefe* and the *Jefita*, after entering the compound with its red brick walls and ivy, walked through the main gate and down a long, cement path past a sign that read "No Talking." The two were allowed in after being frisked and checked for weapons and contraband in a small caged room. The *Jefe* was interested in asking why they checked his pant legs and the tops of his shoes.

Near a sign that read:

> **Inmate Interviews**
> **915am to 1045am**
> **1245pm to 4pm**
> **Billfolds only**
> **No cameras**

The *Jefe* and the *Jefita* later waited patiently at the gate to the bunk-houses and the office designated as the visitor center.

Once inside they waited and sat without words. The *Jefe* leaned against the wall and the *Jefita* sat down at one of the long cafeteria-style tables and bench seats. The *Jefe* was impatient and fought the urge to smoke. The *Jefita* ordered her purse, putting back what a guard had just searched. They both remarked about the windows that were barred over and how every door of the building locked behind them and required a guard.

"How could anyone survive here?" the *Jefita* murmured under her breath.

"The old man Ortiz said this is where Mitedio would land," the *Jefe* whispered in answer. The *Jefita* stared blankly and slowly nodded. "He knew."

As soon as the man entered he was frisked and the bottoms of his shoes were double-checked. The *Jefe* shook his head solemnly. When Mitedio took off his hat and sat at the table, the *Jefe* stood a bit straighter and the *Jefita* sat up in her seat. Mitedio looked comfortable in his Canon City blues, but the *Jefita* noticed how his pant legs had a black stripe down the side and the cuffs of his pants were folded over and yet still dragged on the institutional flooring. Mitedio was the first to speak: "Well, it's the family come to check on my teeth."

"How much time, Mitedio?" *Jefe* asked sharply.

"A nickel," Mitedio said.

"Five years," the *Jefe* repeated and then whistled under his tongue. "Tried to help you out, brother."

"Don't start your shit, Bro," Mitedio snapped.

"It just finally added up for you."

"Don't start nothing, Santiago," the *Jefita* argued. "We came here to see how you're getting along, Mitedio."

Mitedio smiled and reached for his sister-in-law's hand.

"No touching, Ortiz," the *whetto* guard declared.

"How's my boys, Cordelia?" Mitedio asked.

"They miss you and talk about you all the time. They're out in the truck. Won't allow them in."

"Their *Jefe* keeping them busy?" Mitedio asked.

"I keep them busy," the *Jefe* said.

"Yes, Mitedio," the *Jefita* answered. "Their side-jobs, you know."

"You and your Goddamn side-jobs, Brother. You got a job and you're making dollar bills and tonnage and shit."

"Don't give me no advice, Mitedio. You don't have no place to tell me about how to work or raise a boy. You never could keep a job."

"Santiago!" the *Jefita* interrupted.

"What's going on here?" the round-faced guard asked. "This interview needs to end."

The man's words stopped the family; it seemed to surprise them they were being monitored.

"No problem, Sir," the *Jefita* said. "Just family business, Sir."

She smiled and looked conciliatory and hopeful for the guard's patience. She had her hands together and nearly prayed as in her beloved St Francis Church. The sweat began to roll down her wide cheeks. She wiped at her forehead with her handkerchief.

And maybe it was the stress of the day or the child growing inside of her but her stomach began to churn again. The reflex to vomit came upon her and her lips became tight with the waves of nausea before she recovered.

"What would your Mother say of you two? I'm sick of this fighting, Santiago," the *Jefita* pleaded, and the tears built in her eyes and she began to rub at her belly deeply with her thumbs and palms.

"I've seen you two go at it and fight and nothing like brothers are supposed to be," the *Jefita* preached. "I wish I had a brother who would come and see me and come and talk. Can't we even visit for a minute like a family? What kind of men are you?"

The two men stayed silent with their frustration.

"This is the only brother you have, Santiago," the *Jefita* said. "Once he's gone that is it. You've got no one else. And the same goes to you, Mitedio." She fought the continuing urge to gag.

"You okay?" the *Jefe* asked his wife.

"What's wrong with you?" Mitedio wondered. "She pregnant? You pregnant? I wouldn't have hit you if I knew you were pregnant."

By 11 o'clock and somewhere around Fremont County the crew of boys started in. And the *Jefe* hated questions.

"He's sorry and he's thinking over what he's done, boys," the *Jefita* answered.

And then later little Neto let it slip: "He only did what he did because the *Jefe* put him out the house."

"What'd you say, boy?" the *Jefe* barked, hitching himself back and forth in his seat. He reached for Neto with his free hand.

"Let the boys, be, Santiago," the *Jefita* answered, holding her son tightly against her chest. "You know your *Tio* was bad and had to go away. Men don't do them things."

"He stole," Relles added.

"Yes, Relles," the *Jefita* continued. "He stole and had to pay for what he'd done."

The *Jefe* decided to smoke his nasty *cigarillos* and blew the smoke all over the interior of the *truckito*.

The *Jefe* lectured, "A man has to work for what he wants and for what he needs, boys. If I teach you anything it's that. You hear me, boys? You hear me?"

Later that night as the house slept, Neto muffled his tears into the case of his pillow. At first he thought of rising and riding down to the east side for his lost *Tio* Mitedio. He wondered how far Canyon City could be. If he could, he would travel there on his bicycle, to be with the man but he knew that wasn't possible, he knew the *Jefe* would never allow him go. He pulled out Mitedio's magazine with the glossy breasts and nakedness and just stared along with the flashlight.

14. LAUNDROMAT STORY

An all-night Laundromat just behind the golden arches of a McDon-ald's and a Sinclair station stood as the only life for miles along the interstate. At first I thought the lights were a sad hallucination, but I pulled the Monte Carlo into the parking lot on 13" rims after a heavy and wet snowfall. My shirt sopped wet against my skin because the damned driver-side window wouldn't roll up. It happened to be the day before Thanksgiving, even though it felt more like Halloween, and the strange sky that night had just opened up with a small sickle cell of a moon.

For the most part, the story is that I had been out haunting parked cars and neighborhoods, looking for the men that had attacked me, who had produced the black eye and the bashed forehead.

The two kids and I had an unspoken camaraderie before I had even gone into the place, before I started my laundry, before I even met their mother. Through the walls of glass appeared miserable and fogged up, I could only see their round faces. At first I was nervous about going in, but I wanted to get out of the cold, and the kids signaled to me with fingerprints and nose prints on the foggy glass.

Inside, the place smelled of floor cleaner. Washers churned. My jaw ached and my face strained to adjust to the fluorescent lighting. It signaled to me: 30lb Washers/ Save Soap/ Save Quarters.

I wanted to acknowledge the kids right away. They both had dark hair and were dressed shabbily. The crusted mucus on the little girl's nose and the boy's missing high top. The little purse she had and the boy's toy cars. It was all so familiar.

They climbed over the long stretch of white machines, dirtying their hands and the boy's white t-shirt. For a while they were just run-ning and later they took turns locking each other in a dryer, holding the door shut on one another.

I stretched out my two pairs of jeans and the t-shirt I was wearing on the tops of the washers and lay down on the counters, not caring if I slept or if I died. I pulled out a cigarette and lit it casually. I found my shirt had blood on it. It was just after midnight when I noticed that the two little kids and their bucket of chicken belonged to someone.

The mother was on the pay phone. Most of what she said was in Spanish, which I regretted, and it's taken me a while to really translate it all out in my head. "Yah. I'm with the kids. I've got 'em in the laundry with me. Yah, well, what else would I do with them, *Cabróna*?" She shook her head and her long straight hair, half of a Camel tucked neatly behind her ear. She was a big woman of the *llano*, maybe in her forties, wearing tight, red jeans, and the tiniest belly shirt slit down her large front exposing a tremendous bosom. "No, I told you, I don't have a ride. Can't stay here all night," she repeated over and over again. "Can't stay here all night."

I remember I had a greasy bag of burgers and fries from the Mc-Donald's that reminded me of the rain in Macedonia, the lonesomeness of everything you own being wet through and heavy. And they looked so sad, the kids, I mean, like a couple of saints, so I couldn't help but lean way over and drop the bag in between them.

The son had a sloppy crew cut with an awful rat's tail down his back. He had a mouth full of yellow teeth and couldn't stop smiling stupidly as he threw pennies, targeting the reflection of my smiling face in the dryer doors. After several loud screams of direction from their mother the kids finally sat and ate. The boy sat on the concrete floor eating and didn't touch any of my fries. Later, he climbed up into one of the dryers, shutting the door behind. This silent kid just smiled and stared at me from behind the closed glass.

A few less-than-conscious moments later, the little girl shook me into sitting up and for a moment I couldn't quite tell what was memory or what was real. I was still on the washers trying to sleep.

Her dark green eyes gave me a quiet look all serious and thoughtful. She wiped her filthy hands and precious mouth along the front of her sunflower-printed dress. She handed me one of the pennies that her brother had fired towards her head. I smiled and took the greasy penny from her little flawless hands.

The first woman to talk, the one who looked like someone's *Abuelita* and who had no teeth in her mouth, asked me how much time the dryers gave you per quarter. I scraped on a newly dried t-shirt over my head, and she huffed when I told her, "Years." Another woman with glasses seemed to be staring right at me, everything a reaction to me. Sometimes I was prone to forgetting. How I look, I mean. I guess I should always remember but times like these I am prone to forgetting, to dozing off.

Anyway, I did forget as I was listening to this lady. I didn't hear right away when she told me not to smoke. When she told me to think of other people.

The other woman at the end of the long, rectangular building wasn't much better. She was wearing black stretch pants that ran down her snake-like legs into cowboy boots. The purse was just big enough for her cigarettes and Bic and her car keys.

"I hate coming down here. Wish I owned my own. I hate the element."

My mind was like a light bulb breaking.

"I asked you if you were from Fort Carson. Are you from Fort Carson?" she asked me, or someone just like her asked me. I was wearing a 7th Infantry Mountain Post t-shirt. I forgot I had that left in my life."Are you a soldier, young man? Are you from Fort Carson?"

"I was thinkin' you could help me with some money," the mother said to me. "Husband put me out." She balanced herself on platform shoes, between the washers and the dryers.

I had no more money. Everything had already gone into the machines. I'd drunk some too and was relying on a half tank of gas and a crumpled twenty-dollar bill to make it out to California, to Culver City. I hated to think about my own story, much less anyone else's.

For a minute I didn't think there would be anything else other than those few words. I nodded and said, "Your girl's cute." The little girl at this point was sucking on her fingers and the remains of some pink nail polish. "What's her name?"

"Cinnamon."

"Sounds like a porn star name."

She was wiping her daughter's face with spit and a napkin she had pulled from an oversized bag. "Don't know me. Can't talk to me like that."

"I didn't mean to knock you. I have a car outside."

She was folding more clothes, the children's clothes, but she looked out toward the parking lot, and then she gave me a look to size me up. "Got my brother coming."

The mother told me the boy's name was Tenok and I laughed.

"It's Mayan! I wanted to name him something Mayan."

It had been a while since I mouthed the words, since I had to explain who I was to anybody. "Ortiz."

"What?"

"My name is Relles Ortiz."

She looked me straight in the eyes. "See? I could make fun or say something stupid but it's your name. And I ain't going to."

I looked at my shoes.

"Don't care what you say, do you? Can't be like that to people. No one teach you respect? You don't know me from anyone and you want me to get into a car with you when you're obviously not right in the head." She was shaking her head. "That's why you all swole up." And that's when she laughed at me.

She nodded proudly, "Tenok is Mayan." The boy suddenly ran up. "I ain't fuckin stupid."

I nodded.

"Yeah," she said. She scooped up her squirming son and held him and sort of bounced with him making him much younger than he probably was. "Little shit looks just like his old man, too. The bastard. And he used to ride down in Telmpua sometimes. That's where we used to live. They have rodeos for weeks on end down there. It's like religion." She gave a little thimble-sized sigh.

I'd never heard of the place, but I agreed and told her it was beautiful.

"Better than this fuckin place."

"Colorado isn't so bad. I mean, is it?"

"Look around this bitch and tell me that." She just about hung her head as if she had just come to the realization herself.

"Well, that's because it's winter. The state's green in the summer, closer to the mountains, I mean."

I put the twenty-dollar bill I kept in my sock into her hands. She smiled and I thought she was going to cry.

"Hey, you got anything to smoke?" she asked tenderly before tucking her long black hair behind both ears.

And the men that had attacked me, I forgot about the men that attacked me. I never saw them coming, either. I was in a bar called the Whitehorse looking for my *Tio* Neto and I couldn't find that shitty place again if I tried, but I do remember trying to make time with an eighteen-year-old from Albuquerque. She was wearing a scarf around her neck printed with small hearts on it, I can remember that much. My brother Romes and his pills were long gone and by this point I felt like a stone skipped along the water.

This girl had been singing along to the jukebox for what seemed like an eternity, which is how she caught my attention, saved me, really. She wanted nothing to do with me and she obviously felt no pain because she was fucking up the easiest of lines.

"Bottle up and explode, over and over! Bottle up and explode!"

When she did finally land up talking to me, though, which was more about boredom than attraction, she couldn't stop talking about her father and how he was a Christian. She said her father told her the Devil makes us drink, that that's how he gets into our actions.

While she was in a booth across from me, she told me her name but I couldn't pronounce it as hard as I tried. And then I found out that her father was dead-meat like mine. And that's when she asked me if I believed in God. She told me how she used to think that only by believing in Him would we be saved. That's why she had a crucifix tattooed on her chest above her tits. I had no idea what she was saying because I'm not religious, but she had the deepest, most amazing green eyes like my wife. There was a small blemish on her face where her boyfriend had taken a cigarette to her about a month earlier or maybe it was a pockmark, I can't be certain, but she kept checking it in the mirror behind the bar.

"Buy me a drink. They won't sell me anymore," she told me. And I did once, and then again and then a third time. And then after the sea of rum and RC Colas, she preached to me: "God told Job that the world has to be nasty sometimes. Can't be perfect everywhere, you know? It just can't be." She was drunker than me, drunker than anyone in the place, almost in slow motion. She said, "I mean that alone leads me to think that there's got to be more going on, going on behind the scenes, you know? You know?"

"God's a fuckin' prick."

"Yes," she said. "Yes. That's my point. That's exactly the point, you know?"

But I didn't know, and this continued out into the parking lot until just before she was about to get into my Chevy and show me more of those tattoos on her chest. Until this fuck she had been dating and his crew rolled up on us. And this is the part of that night I wish I could say wasn't clear, that I can say proved anything about myself or who I was becoming. But I can't say that.

The story is really about the mother with the two kids. Later that night, I was out in my car with her, smoking my dog shit from New Mexico and trying to put my hand down the front of her pants. I was trying to get her to come to the Whitehorse with me, to drive all over town. She wasn't having any of it.

We smoked the last of my dog shit out of a pipe whose filter was pretty much dirtied up. Her hair smelled like peaches and her skin was becoming darker and lovelier.

She looted around her purse and finally dumped the contents out next to me. She showed me a picture of her husband Javier. He was in full *Charo* garb out on a *llano* somewhere on a pale gray and spotted horse straight out of a Clint Eastwood movie, the leather a bright red and ornate. His hat was in his hand over his head. His face wore a bearded smirk.

"The Lone Ranger," I said, serious as hell. The mother laughed and her large breasts shook. For the first time she moved in closer to me. We were just about holding each other.

I remember thinking that if someone were to see us in this Monte Carlo, if someone were walking by they would think we were happy.

"So why do you think he left?"

"Don't know."

"You can't think of even a little reason?"

"Cuz he's a *pendejo*, I guess."

"Really? That's what you think?" For a while I left the car running so she wasn't so cold. The window I could roll up started to fog over and gave us quite a bit of privacy. I wanted to kiss her and tell her to come with me, but I had no idea how to take care of myself, much less her. I asked her about what she remembered.

"The fuck you sayin'?" She gave me a look, like it was the first time she looked at anything. "Never heard questions like these," she said. "Shouldn't worry about the past. Should worry about you."

I couldn't make sense, make her understand.

She had a look in her eye and no emotion on her face. She was higher than high, laughing and sort of crying. She didn't care what I said or did, and then, before I tried my damnedest to kiss her, she said, "Sometimes we choose shit and it don't just happen to us, Army. I hate to tell you." My head went down and the static in my inner ear failed.

I was the first one to fall asleep.

The sky that next morning was a brilliant light blue and gray, and warm sunlight filled the car like a policeman's flashlight, the ground covered white with a fresh snow. The car was freezing and smelled of old cigarettes and pine air freshener. We were out in the parking lot, I could tell by the sound of the cars, but for a minute I wasn't sure where I was in time and space.

And then the mother screamed, and the sound sort of carved into me, cleared my head. It came to me right through the open window. It was so beautiful and definite, like the emptiness inside of me. It was about six forty-five in the morning and my last view of her was out in a southern Colorado morning, searching for my little girl and the boy.

15. THE HOUSE OF ORDER

Neto rides out to a bar called The Hideaway, a dark place with a dance floor the size of a welcome mat. His beloved Freya Lynn kisses Joseph Vigil and so he drains rum and RC Cola all night. He misses curfew. His face covers in tears and he speaks soft, damning words to himself. He yells out for her and grabs for what is around him. The next morning in the smelly darkness of his third floor room, he hunches in a ball on the floor and cries. Shivering, Neto waits patiently after he drives the needle through the flesh of his arm until he hallucinates soft kisses down his spine.

His sponsor tells him that he isn't a man. That he could never be a man without respecting his family, without respecting the house rules.

"Ernesto Ortiz," Bob Wilson lectures. "We are all good men in here. We all have the power to do better."

Neto stares. His mouth drops open with boredom.

"Every hardship we live through will lead us to becoming stronger," Bob says.

This afternoon Neto is taking an especially ferocious attack because his stash has been found out. He feels sick and achy. Bob promises not to contact Neto's PO as long as Neto promises to attend "group" and not leave the property for at least three weeks other than to work.

"I am not blind, Ernesto. I am giving you every benefit of the doubt." He looks directly at Neto. "I know what you say about these sessions. I know what you think."

"What do I think?"

Bob says, "You think I don't know why you do the things you do and say the things you say."

Neto almost laughs out loud. And so do the other men at the meeting. He tries to hold on to their names: Bob Apples, Mickey Torrez, Something Smith, and No-Named Archuleta.

"You think I don't know the pain you feel," Bob repeats. "I used to be just like you, Ernesto. I am your Christian brother. I had everything once. I had a home and a wife. I had a teaching job and I had a car. It was a Chevy. And I had money in the bank but I had nothing. More nothing than you have right now. Until I found Jesus."

Everyone at the meeting is silent, careless. No one could remember Bob revealing so much in these afternoon meetings. But after finding Neto on the floor the place is pretty shaken up. Bob's authority is pretty shaken up.

Bob continues: "I was afraid to be seen and I was afraid to get through the day. Afraid to admit what I was. And I was afraid every-body would see me. I know that's what you're afraid of, Ernesto. And I am telling you God is here for you. I see your crucifix on your neck, Ernesto. I know you know what I am talking about."

"I know what you are talking about," No-Named says. "I don't want to be seen."

"Thank you, No-Named. Today, though, we are focusing on Er-nesto."

"Let him talk if he wants to talk," Neto says.

"Ernesto, I am the director of this meeting," Bob says. He can feel the meeting becoming cracked open right down the middle and a thou-sand baby spiders crawling out over the community room floor.

"Well, that's what we supposed to do here, ain't it? Neto says. "We're supposed to talk."

"Yeah," someone says and a few others repeat it.

Neto told me the residents named the building the Highland, after the street it was built on in downtown Colorado Springs, and that later, in the 70's, some state agency changed it to Pikes Peak Health Hori-zons. But Neto always referred to it as the house of order. The place to get your habits straightened out. The red brick mother of a build-ing was in poor condition, and in the past fifteen years he had lived in several halfway houses, friend's homes, and girlfriends' apartments, and for a time he lived with his cousin Tino in Denver. He lived with nieces and nephews on sofas and fold-out beds, and he had lived in five hostels since his girl Freya Lynn put him out of her house in Colorado Springs. Nothing compared to the Highland.

From his window at the Highland he looked out at the sacred pow-er mountain of the Utes that was Pikes Peak, a mountain looming always to the west of the city, and littered with businesses and chim-neys, the low roofs of hotels and residences cutting into the view of the Navajo red foothills and absolutely jagged hills and green lowlands. His window was high and his room was narrow, and from his room the stream of pigeons and the sounds of downtown trains and buses filled his inner ear and woke him at midnight and at three and again at five. His shades were frayed and tattered and did not keep out sunlight or the moonlight. The room had a single, bare light bulb and the walls were thin and could not keep out the sound of the neighbors' slamming doors, arguments, snores or hacking coughs.

Neto Ortiz had no intention of staying on at the Highland. He continued to pack his clean laundry into his duffel bag, readying for his exit date and his moving to better living conditions, readying to run from his sentences.

I find him in Denver, on the 5-North wing of the VA Hospital off of Colorado Boulevard resting on sheets frayed around the ends and stamped:

> **Department of Veteran Affairs**
> **United States of America**
> **Government Property**
> **Not For Sale.**

"*Cabrón*," he says. "You just looking all over for me, huh?"

"How you feeling?"

"I'm all right, *Hijo*," he says, slapping my hand. He keeps rubbing at his chin and his unkempt head of hair. "Nothing's wrong. Nothing. Who told you something's wrong? Who told you that?"

"You're in the hospital, *Tio*."

Neto laughs and winces as he shifts his weight. "This catheter pinches my *verga*, you know."

His hair has grown out quite a bit and makes him look like a rough old Chicano. His body has changed from the hulk of a man I remember in my youth to a sickly 140 pounds. His arms are thick and sore, a row of adhesive tape clasping the IV and the tubes to his skin. His arms look cut and bandaged and his legs look thin and weak. He is shirtless and he has a crucifix hanging around his neck.

He finally tells me he was sober for most of those years I was away and that he held jobs in New Mexico and here in Denver, Colorado where the new wife sobered him up. The living situation worked well for Neto until he received the divorce papers. Things like that were always happening to us.

A year later Neto celebrated a third divorce with a three week drinking binge that led to his 5th DUI, which equals felony status in Arapahoe County. He cheated going to jail for months because the county made a clerical error and lost the paperwork for two of those charges, but it turned over the whole life he had made in New Mexico.

He moved right out of his girlfriend's house, into city jail for eighteen months, and then into a halfway house for six.

An elderly woman with a hearing aid, her face dark and puffy, walks into Neto's hospital room and gives him a bag of toiletries and a small bible. Her name is Tilly Mendoza and she is patting Neto softly on the shoulder. "You a good Catholic boy, Ortiz," she says.

"You're the only one in here who talks to me decent. These damn *gabacho* doctors."

"They'll take care of you. They do good work in here."

"They ain't fair about the pain medication."

"Life ain't fair, *Hijo*," she says with a seriousness. "If life was fair, the horse would ride half the time, no?" She puts her hand on his side, approximating where his kidney should be. "You in good shape," she says and I start to get the feeling she tells everyone the same story. "Just stay away from the tobacco. That tobacco will tear you down, *Hijo*. And the wine. Stay away from the wine. My father used to drink the wine. No beer, just wine."

She looks right into my eyes and then she winks.

"I know we got a strong one here," she says, giving Neto one last pat on the shoulder.

Later, a twelve-year-old doctor comes in and goes over his entire medical file, and then Neto receives a prayer from another woman volunteer. With tears forming in his eyes, he watches as she reads the prayer. "Peace be with you," the woman tells us.

Neto is living off of Colfax Avenue and I have to make several U-turns because of the parking situation and also because Neto can't remember his own exact address. I thought we'd have to drive all over town if not for his sudden memory of the street. We go past Carter Avenue and find the place. Looks like a one-room apartment buried in a sea of one-room apartments. Neto has no car and no income except for a small social security check and even smaller VA benefits, and the place looks it. Reminds me of the old neighborhood though I don't tell Neto any of this.

As we walk to the door a young girl and boy are throwing handfuls of rocks towards the parking lots and windshields. They barely stop for a second as we pass. Neto laughs and blows smoke from a cigarette around them and throws his *vacha* down.

He explains that months back he felt at his chest and couldn't breathe, decided to walk to the bus stop down the block. He points at the spot where they found him. The doctors told him it was a minor heart attack brought on by the many meds he takes for his one remaining kidney. They told him he needs to stop smoking and drinking. Told him to take it easy and watch his diet and meds.

"I could of called the 911," he tells me. "But no money, Manito."

"You could have died on the street, *Tio*."

He says, "It will all be yesteryear soon." And to this I have no idea what to say. I nod.

Neto stands in his apartment and takes off the shirt he is wearing and places it into the garbage bag, then takes another from the bag and pulls it over his head. There is a ripped pocket over his heart and a hole just near the stretched collar. I recognize a few of the collared shirts I gave him years back before a cousin's wedding when I was afraid he would wear a Denver Bronco jersey.

The living room has three sofas and the room smells of mold and cat piss, though I see no cat. I notice exactly what is missing. There is no television and no walls between the bathroom and the bedroom or the kitchen. There are no bookcases, lamps or clocks. No appliances on the counter except for a hotplate and nothing covering the bare cement floors. There are no newspapers or magazines, no bird in the birdcage. There is no telephone and no closet.

I ask him, "You got a cat, *Tio*?"

"Damn thing ran off."

What Neto does have are glorious photos, several large framed shots saved from the *Abuelita's* albums.

Abuelito Santiago and *Abuelita* Cordelia on their wedding day, the young man in his Army dress uniform and the young woman in a white lace dress.

Mitedio Ortiz when he is in his twenties, which looks like a black-and-white photo that's been hand colored, like they used to back in the day before there were color photos.

There is a large one of cousin Ricardo on his wedding day standing with Neto in front of the Alibi Bar and Grill in Huérfano County.

Neto introduces a photo of an old woman as his Great Grandmother from New Mexico. "Full blooded Navajo," he tells me, like he is letting me in on a secret. There is also a lone photo of my mother from back in the day. She's in a cheerleading outfit standing out front of Central High.

There is no sign of Neto's brother, Relles. I double check the apartment walls as Neto pisses into the toilet bowl across from the sofa.

Next comes one of those moments. I see a plaster figure of *La Vir-*

gen de Guadalupe. The same Mary from the *Abuelitos'* backyard, right from the old neighborhood. The plaster is cracking and the golden rope around her waist is frayed and fading. Her hands are clasped and a few fingers from her left hand are missing.

I ask, "What are you gonna do with her, *Tio*?"

"Take it. It don't mean nothing to me no more. Take it. It never did nothing for me. Take it now."

I wrap *La Virgen* in a blanket that smells of cigarette smoke and carry her out to my borrowed Chevy. I gently lower her down into the trunk on top of the spare tire.

I couldn't refuse driving him to his old haunts. He hasn't been down south or around Colorado Springs since the new wife put him out, and he needs someone to drive him to visit friends and family out on West Avenue. Needs someone to cash a disability check for him. Needs someone to pay for the gas.

Down stairs carpeted with rubber treads and past fake wood paneling, we tour a subterranean place called the Shanghai Lounge where he supposedly met a girlfriend named Miranda years before. Then he takes me to Valesco's Diner out toward Arapahoe County, where we sit down in front of a broken down counter straight out of the 1950's. We face two tired waitresses and a kid cleaning up tables.

I am introduced to Valesco, as the man flips omelet orders, fried potatoes and pancakes on the ancient looking grill. Jorge coughs and yells, shakes his finger at Neto and then slaps his hand.

"You look too damn skinny," Valesco says as he slows to talk with us. He wears pale gray fatigues and a wife-beater t-shirt underneath a greasy apron. "You'll have to sit here and eat, *Cabrón*. Have a few beers. Put on a few pounds."

"He ain't like me," Neto says. "Little man's all grown up. Headed to college. He's got what it takes, you know."

Valesco has three or four orders going and I am envious of how the man can speak and joke while getting food out on narrow plates and thumbing through order tickets from those two waitresses.

"I hope you keeping your *Tio* straight," Valesco says. "Nobody else can, *pocho*. But maybe you can try, no?"

In a booth near the plate-glass window that looks out on to the old highway, Neto is talkative and loud. I notice his forehead is longer and he still has his hospital ID around his wrist. My *Tio* Neto drains two tall drafts and gives me some of Valesco's bud wrapped in tin foil. I tell him to go easy. He points out each hole in the gums for each tooth he had removed while in jail. What teeth he has left look rotted and stained.

He hands me one of my father's dog tags. I hold the smooth metal in my hand and read the stamped letters:

> **ORTIZ**
> **RELLES J**
> **US 55874642**
> **O POS**
> **Catholic.**

"Your Relles was a good man," Neto says. "A Goddamn real-life Vietnam hero."

Later I have to interrupt the old stories to say, "I'm going to have a daughter. Inez stopped taking birth control."

"Inez is the school teacher, no? With the fat ass?"

"Another kid would make two." I hold up two fingers before I slip the dog tag away and light another cigarette with the last cigarette. "I'm saying I can't stay away too long, *Tio*. I gotta get back to her." I get just a touch of comprehension from him, or I only imagine it. He seems to only want and talk about the past.

We pull out of the place and enter the purple Monte Carlo, bounding down Interstate 25 from Colorado Springs to drop him off in Huérfano County. We stop in almost every bar and dive Neto can remember. I have so much time with him. I don't know what to ask or how to ask him.

The owner of this one joint is turning around the open sign and we are back in the car. We both are too drunk to be driving. I admit the girlfriend doesn't want me drinking like this and he finally agrees. The engine is crying from overheating and we limp up and down those strange interstates.

I phone Neto only one other time not too many years later when college is all done and behind me, and when we speak he is quick to think I want money or a place to stay. I break down and try to tell him more about Inez and the daughter. He reminds me he is an old man, reminds me I am still young. "I don't know, Manito. All I can tell you is stay away from places like the Highland." He drunkenly tells me as the line goes dead, "Try and save all those troubles."

16. FARMHOUSE IN THE LANES

That afternoon the sun came down hard, but the wind came underneath, from the open *llano*. Along with oppressive dust and force as the truck moved over unpaved lanes beyond Blende, Colorado, and it seemed to cool the old man's sweaty face and neck if only for a moment. As far as the old man could see the lanes outside the passenger side window held multiple tracks and ruts but no footprints.

"This is a damn day for the sun, Manito," the *Abuelito* Ortiz said. He pulled his handkerchief from his overall pocket, wiped at his burnt neck and set his arm on the exposed metal of the truck's hot door. As the young boy steered the Ford up the long slope of 27th Lane he looked back across the onion fields to where the old Montoya Farm and the old Musso's Farm blew up their perpetual white dust, and on down to the western roadway towards the horizon and the highway to La Junta and Las Animas. Just across the *campos*, the blue Colorado sky was like a canvas propped over the hills and the remote houses of the valley.

"It wouldn't be so bad if it wasn't for the heat," the boy said without looking at the old man, choosing to focus on the road and the destination ahead.

The old man continued to look out towards the western horizon. "This all belonged to the Montoyas and the lettuce farmers," he said. "We picked out here when the steel mill was on strike back in '59. I ever tell you?"

"You talk to me and I got to watch the road. I don't like to drive when the dust is high like this, *Jefe*."

The old man glanced over at the boy who was struggling with the oversized steering wheel and the tree shifter. "You got good eyes, Manito," the old man said. "When you're young you got good eyes. But I drove these roads all my life, Manito, and I'll tell you when the road curves. I'll tell you."

"I know."

"I used to drive out here when I worked for the Musso farm. Already had been driving for years when I was your age, Manito. Bringing home money."

"You told me," the boy said.

They passed an abandoned farm, with a long meadow where two geldings were running along the fence line downhill between Spruce trees.

"A man could make a living in those days," the old man said. "Could earn a wage and pay rent and have money left over for a drink and for a woman."

The boy nodded and shifted, making the transmission groan and grind as the clutch popped.

"Don't have to shift so much, Manito," the old man said. "Let the engine go until you lose speed. The engine knows what to do and she'll tell you."

"I know."

"Then do it, *Cabrón*. I only got one truck and I want to keep it, no?" The old man drummed on the door, grinning and then laughing to himself at the way the boy never took his eyes from the road when he talked. The way he overcompensated for each curve and bump.

The boy took his foot off the gas and shifted. "Maybe you should drive, *Jefe*. I don't have a license."

"Keep going, Manito. How do you learn the way unless you do it, you know?"

The old man freed a cigarette from the pack in his overall pocket. He tamped the end before settling it just under his moustache on the edge of his leathered lips. He tried the dash lighter and then struck a match from a book in the glove compartment. The dark smoke spilled from his nostrils as he stared at the wild daisies and the wild grass growing in the lush fields and the shaded places, the dense weeds and the cactus building into the dense brush along the roadside. Just as the boy shifted again the truck crawled out onto a side road near an abandoned farmhouse.

"See that *casita*, Manito?" the old man said. "That thing will stand there for years and years if you didn't mess with it. I know the Maldanados who built it. I worked with them. I know all these houses. He was a carpenter and built that house with his sons and nephews. That's how they did it in those days. *Familia*."

The boy pulled off the road into the long grass just behind the farmhouse. The brakes cried as the ride lurched to a stop. The air was warm and filled with the smell of heavy timber, and crickets were chanting in the heat. The old man inhaled and filled the small compartment with the pungent smell of smoke. He leaned out the wide window and spit onto the edge of his *cigarillo* before throwing the *vacha*. The old man stretched his muscles and made his bones crack. He stepped out to look across the broken walls and boards of the farmhouse that disappeared down into a deep brush.

"A man could lay down in the shade here on the side of the house and just sleep real nice," the old man said. "If I lay down, Manito, will you do all the work for me?"

"Shoot." With a bucket of tools in his hand, the boy looked at him with respect and seriousness. He was prepared for the day of work ahead. "You shouldn't be out in this heat anyway." The boy looked at the old man as if he wasn't quite sure if he was joking but he was willing to do whatever his *Abuelito* said.

The boy had been that way since his father died and ever since his mother never returned from California. If the old man sat down, the boy brought his newspaper and his reading glasses. If the old man yawned and napped in his favorite chair in the living room, the boy covered him and took the pipe from his teeth. If he was hungry the boy would peel potatoes and warm tortillas. It was all he had ever known to do.

After gauging the farmhouse and the surrounding scenery the old man reached in and got his thermos of coffee in one hand and his tool box with the other. He also grabbed at his lunchbox and an old blanket, struggling to place the necessities of the day under each arm.

"I'm not so old, Manito," the old man said. "I'm not ready for the coffin just yet. Think the world had killed me since the steel mill?"

"I know. You still got it." The boy nested the toolbox, hooked his arm through the lunchbox and then slung the blanket over his shoulder, took the thermos away from the old man. "Here. Give me some of them tools."

All the way around the farmhouse and up the road the wind kicked up dirt under their feet.

"Nobody been around here in a while, Manito," the old man said. "You can tell by the tracks."

"No tracks on the side road neither."

"*Oy lo. Muy chingon.* What, are you a tracker now? *Muy* Kit Carson. They teach you that in school?"

"They don't teach me nothing in school, Grampo. I learn more riding with you and *Tio* Neto."

All the way up the road to the farmhouse the old man jerked his head at the perimeter, nervously and guiltily.

"Think somebody will come up on us, *Jefe?*"

"No one comes out here," the old man said. "Don't nobody give a shit about this building. Nobody even knows it's out here no more."

"Be nice if nobody gives us no problems."

"Nobody going to give us no problems, Manito. This is my land. I own this bit of land, Manito. I pay the taxes. It's mine."

The boy nodded his head and listened intently. He acted as if he knew this answer the whole way out from town.

"This farmhouse and the wood is all mine," the old man said. "As far as I figure it."

They came out in front of the building to what looked like a meadow of weeds and rusted car bodies. The farmhouse that had once stood proudly was now a ruined foundation overgrown with weeds and roots. The flood of 1964 had scooped a path a hundred yards long near the front. Nearby tree trunks crisscrossed the area; some trees were dead and others looked half-dead.

"I've got my mind ready for some work, Manito," the old man said. "We can get some good money for some of this lumber. Not much here but what we can pull down will give us some nice pay."

The boy nodded.

"You'll be eating steak tonight, Manito."

The boy was inspecting the boards and the ancient wood. "There's nails too, *Jefe*. Should we get the nails?"

"The wood is what I'm interested in, Manito."

Before the boy could say anything the old man had stripped down to the white undershirt and was hammering out rusted nails and prying at boards.

By the time half of the truck bed was full, the heat had worsened but the wind had shifted so that the west side of the farmhouse cut most of it off and it was cool in the long shade. They went deeper into the shade by the foundation and ate lunch and drank sweetened coffee from the thermos. Then the boy struggled down on to the blanket, laid over the hard ground and whistled playfully, as he looked up at the sky. The old man sat on top of broken foundation and drank at the mason jar of water. The wind came in through the open shafts where the boards had been stripped and taken down. Down the view the farmhouse once held, the *campos* looked like great rolling plains of brown and scattered greens. Out towards the small town of Blende the houses were white and red cubes on the horizon strung far out on a small string of road.

"I used to take your father out here," the old man said.

"I know. My homeboy Neto tells me everything."

And then the old man slapped the boy's head, connected with a pretty vicious open hand slap that made the boy's head jerk. "Your *Tio* was never worth a damn for work," the old man said.

The boy looked down and didn't say a word. He kept the tears deep inside of him.

"I'm telling you about your father. Neto's not your father." The old man then handed the jar of cool water to the boy. "What'll you do when I'm not around to tell you the truth? Seems like half the people in this family forget, you know? I gotta keep it all straight for you, Manito." The old man leaned back and lit another *cigarillo*. He took another drink from the thermos top and then spit some of the coffee out onto the hard clay. "Soon I'll never be able tell you these things. I'm old, Manito. I used to work all day from early till the sun came down and then I would pull up the headlights from the truck and keep going. I could make deliveries up and down the lanes here to every farm and ranch around here with only a bottle of ice water with me, Manito."

The old man leaned farther back and the boy could see the strain coming into his face and neck. The old man didn't move or shift his weight but his voice rose sharply and loudly. "All I am saying is watch who you respect, boy," the old man said. "I'm telling you about your father."

"Yes, sir, *Jefe*."

"So don't forget that. Neto my ass, Manito."

"Okay," the boy said.

"That Neto don't even work and he's got kids and no wife. A damn habit."

"Habit", the way he said it, like an incurable disease only leading to one outcome.

"Shit. In my day my father wouldn't have let me steal as much as an apple."

Later the old man lit another *cigarillo* and smiled and coughed up past the falling roof of the farmhouse, up towards the blue sky and the tops of the nearby spruce and maple trees. The old man wheezed and closed his eyes. Soon he was on the ground and dozing and the boy gently took the *cigarillo* from the old man's lips. He took his own slow drag before leaning back against the foundation.

A good hot stiff wind was now shifting and breaking around the two workers. For a long while the boy stood there sweating and staring at the old man's *siesta*. First, he thought of taking the truck and running, slipping away to Neto's duplex and a sea of rum and RC Colas, cartons of cigarettes in the Frigidaire. Then he thought of the tire iron and bashing the old man while he slept to find a small freedom. But out here in the lanes, the boy also thought, it was so quiet and far from everything that can get to you. He quickly knew why the old man liked to drive out here. For a while he sat there and felt his own pulse in his body as he finished up the *cigarillo*. He felt the clouds move overhead and his brow started to cool. And soon there were tears and sobs to choke on until he finally filled his lungs with the odor of heat and dust before heading back to the job of wood and crowbar.

The boy worked very fast, wanting to surprise the old man with the number of boards in the bed of the truck. After an hour, he worked back toward the side where the old man was snoring. He had the truck's bed filled and he was surprised. He liked the coarseness to his hands, the way his sweat-soaked white undershirt felt cool on his skin. Down on his knees he was prying at a stubborn nail when the old man came up quietly behind and watched him struggle to recover the board. The old man leaned in and placed his hand to the boy's shoulder.

"How's it going?" the *Abuelito* said. He had his shirt back on and another *cigarillo* in his mouth.

"I got more on this one to do but I filled the truck, *Jefe*."

"As long as you're working hard, *Mihijo*." The old man watched the boy's arms and the dark skin of his neck covered in sweat, the way the boy gripped the metal crowbar and worked at the rusted nail. "You're doing fine."

OTHER ANAPHORA LITERARY PRESS TITLES

Evidence and Judgment
By Lynn Clarke

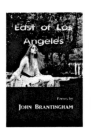

East of Los Angeles
By John Brantingham

Death Is Not the Worst Thing
By T. Anders Carson

The Seventh Messenger
By Carol Costa

Rain, Rain, Go Away...
By Mary Ann Hutchison

Truths of the Heart
By G. L. Rockey

Interviews with BFF Winners
By Anna Faktorovich, Ph.D.

Compartments
By Carol Smallwood

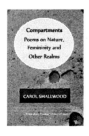

CPSIA information can be obtained at www.ICGtesting.com
Printed in the USA
LVOW040906080212

267705LV00003B/8/P